THE
THROWAWAY
SOCIETY

THE THROWAWAY SOCIETY

BY SALLY LEE

An Impact Book
Franklin Watts
New York/London/Toronto/Sydney
1990

Diagram on page 41 from "Managing Solid Waste" by
Philip R. O'Leary, copyright © 1988 by Scientific American, Inc.
All rights reserved.

Photographs courtesy of: Keep America Beautiful:
pp. 13, 31, 73; Greenpeace: pp. 18 (Bob Brubaker),
99 (Vallette), 102 (Zachary Singer), 118 (Midgley);
Browning-Ferris Industries, Inc.: pp. 24, 52;
Westinghouse Electric Corporation/Resource Energy
Systems Division: p. 53; Al Avenoso: p. 66;
Texas General Land Office: pp. 89, 93, 94;
Clean Houston Inc.: pp. 79, 80.

Library of Congress Cataloging-in-Publication Data

Lee, Sally.
     The throwaway society / by Sally Lee.
         p.   cm.—(An Impact book)
     Includes bibliographical references.
     Summary: Examines the growing problem of how to handle solid
wastes, exploring such areas as collecting and transporting waste,
sanitary landfills, incineration, recycling, and ocean dumping.
     ISBN 0-531-10947-X
     1. Refuse and refuse disposal—United States—Juvenile literature.
2. Pollution—United States—Juvenile literature. [1. Refuse and
refuse disposal.   2. Pollution.] I. Title.
TD788.L43   1990
363.72'8—dc20   90-33027   CIP   AC

CONTENTS

THE
THROWAWAY
SOCIETY

Other books by Sally Lee

DONOR BANKS

NEW THEORIES ON
DIET AND NUTRITION

PREDICTING VIOLENT STORMS

1

IN A HEAP
OF TROUBLE

On March 22, 1987, the tugboat *Break of Dawn* left
New York towing a barge loaded with 3,186 tons of
baled, commercial garbage. The plans for the trip were
simple enough. The garbage would be taken to North
Carolina, where the methane gas that builds up under
garbage when it decays would be extracted. But the
plan ran into a snag when officials in North Carolina
turned the barge away, fearing that it contained hazardous materials.

For two months the wayward barge covered over
5,000 miles (8,000 km) as it wandered from port to port,
looking for a place to unload its unwanted cargo. Ala-
bama, Louisiana, Mississippi, Texas, and Florida all re-
jected requests for the barge to unload in their states.
Mexico, the Bahamas, and the Central American nation
of Belize didn't want the infamous barge in their countries, either. The barge eventually went back to New
York, where it sat for over three months while citizens
and officials argued in court about what to do with it.
Finally, in early September, the trash was burned in a
municipal incinerator in Brooklyn and its ashes buried
in Islip on Long Island, where much of the trash had
been generated.

Although the misadventures of the garbage-laden barge were joked about in the news media, a serious problem was becoming apparent. America is a "throwaway" society and is quickly running out of room to dispose of its trash.

THE THROWAWAY SOCIETY

Trash, solid waste, refuse, rubbish, garbage—no matter what you call it, it's still an unpopular topic. Most people only want to think about it long enough to toss it into the nearest dumpster or haul it to the curb for pickup. Once it is out of sight, it is quickly forgotten. From that point on, most people are quite willing to let someone else worry about it. But in many areas of the country the problem of disposing of the growing piles of garbage is becoming critical and can no longer be ignored.

The United States generates more trash than any other nation on earth, and the amount keeps increasing at an alarming rate. Between 1960 and 1986, the amount of American garbage grew 80 percent from 87.5 million tons to 157.7 million tons annually. That's enough to fill some 63,000 trash trucks each day with a jumbled mass of food wastes, newspapers and magazines, cans and bottles, leaves and lawn clippings, broken toys and appliances, old clothes, dead pets, disposable cups, plates, razor blades and diapers, cosmetic jars and tubes, aerosol cans, rags, rugs, vacuum cleaner sweepings, and a wide variety of other rubbish. That figure doesn't include another 90 million tons of waste generated by industry each year. With that added in, the grand total of America's trash is a whopping 250 million tons a year, according to Environmental Protection Agency (EPA) estimates.

The United States produces more trash per person than any other nation on earth.

REASONS FOR A GROWING PROBLEM

The accumulation of waste in the United States has gotten out of hand for a number of reasons. The first problem is our rapidly growing population. [In 1965, approximately 193 million people lived in the United States. By 1995, that number is expected to be roughly 260 million, an increase of 35 percent in just thirty years.] If the amount of waste each person threw out each day remained the same, there would still be a large increase just because there would be more people to do the throwing. But the problem is worse than that. As our population grows, so does our ability to generate trash.

Over the past century, the United States has grown in affluence as well as in population. Many of our "throwaway" habits can be blamed on this affluence. In addition to our having more money to spend on food and other products, new products are also coming out each day along with enticing commercials to convince us that we need them. Factories are pouring out products that are designed to become obsolete, from 18 billion disposable diapers a year to mountains of computer printouts and masses of Styrofoam food containers. We have become a nation hooked on the convenience of disposable items. Our trash cans are stuffed with paper napkins, towels, and tablecloths, along with disposable pens, razors, and even cameras and contact lenses. With more people in the work force, frozen and carry-out foods (along with their disposable packaging) have replaced many home-cooked meals.

It's not only the products themselves that create the problem; it's also the packaging those products come in. Almost everything we buy comes in cardboard boxes, plastic or paper bags, plastic or Styrofoam cartons, glass bottles and jars, or metal containers. This packaging alone makes up about one-third of the household waste

14

in our waste stream. Much of it is needed to keep the products sanitary and in good condition, but some of it is unnecessary. Unfortunately, the goals of package designers are just the opposite of the goals of waste managers. Packagers want containers that won't burn, break, crush, degrade, or dissolve. This is just what the waste processors *don't* want.

The complexity of the trash has increased along with its amount. Many of the things we throw away today threaten our health and our environment. Glass, aluminum, some plastics, and many other modern products are almost indestructible when they reach the landfill. New developments in the chemical and nuclear industries have led to a generation of toxic wastes that create special health hazards.

Technology doesn't always have to mean an increase in the amount of waste to be disposed of. Other industrialized nations, such as Japan and West Germany, throw away only half as much refuse as does the United States. This shows that it is possible to have a high standard of living and still produce less waste.

RUNNING OUT OF SPACE

While the amount of trash we throw out continues to grow, the places available to put that trash are disappearing. Landfills, which are the final destination for some 86 percent of America's trash, are closing at the rate of almost one a day. In the ten years between 1978 and 1988, an estimated 70 percent of the landfill sites in the United States were closed, leaving the nation with about 5,500 in 1988. The EPA estimates that by 1993 another 2,275 will have closed. Very few new landfills are opening to replace those that have shut down. The EPA predicts that as many as twenty-seven out of the fifty states will have run out of room to dump their garbage by 1990.

Some landfills have been closed because they ran out of room. Others closed when it was discovered that they were contaminating nearby water sources. Stricter regulations governing new landfills and incinerators have increased the expense to the point that many communities are not able to build new ones.

The lack of room for landfills is especially critical in the densely populated northeastern states. Some crowded cities have already run out of room and have to ship their garbage away. The metropolitan area of Philadelphia, with a population of 2 million people, has no landfills left. The city must ship its waste as far away as Ohio and southern Virginia. Since 1980 the cost of handling garbage in Philadelphia has risen from $20 to $90 a ton.

In 1986 Rhode Island decided to no longer accept refuse from other states and closed its dumps to out-of-state trash. For a while it had to put state troopers at the borders to keep garbage trucks from sneaking in.

With a shortage of landfill space, incineration at resource recovery facilities or waste-to-energy plants has become more popular. But the amount of waste handled at these facilities is still small—amounting to only 6 percent of the trash generated in 1986. These facilities are very expensive to build, do not always run properly, and have the potential of polluting the atmosphere with toxic fumes. The ash that remains after incineration may contain a concentration of toxic chemicals that requires special handling.

THE RISING
PRICE TAG

The cost of getting rid of wastes is climbing. Purchasing land for landfills has become extremely expensive, and building environmentally safe incinerators is even more costly. And since these new sites have to be far enough away from residential areas to keep homeowners happy, trash collectors must haul their loads much farther to get to disposal sites. Each extra mile adds to the cost. Also, since there are more hazardous substances in our waste today, safety measures must be taken with landfills and incinerators to safeguard the environment. These factors, combined with the increasing amount of waste generated, make waste disposal very expensive.

Residents of Union County, New Jersey, near New York City, saw their annual collection and dumping costs skyrocket from $70 to $420 per household in just one year. The residents must pay these costs themselves through higher taxes or higher fees paid to private sanitation firms. It is especially difficult for people living in low-income neighborhoods to handle this increase.

The huge amounts of money involved in disposing of refuse and the desperation of some areas to get rid of their trash has encouraged some unscrupulous people to get into the business. The opportunity to cheat is great. At the Meadowlands landfill in New Jersey, fifteen workers spend their time looking for trash that is being brought in illegally from out of the area. They look for return addresses on envelopes and other clues that will indicate that the trash is not local. Haulers are fined if they bring in trash from outside New Jersey.

So many people try to dump illegally in New York that the state now has a task force of armed sanitation police officers that patrol areas frequented by illegal dumpers. When caught, these lawbreakers are fined and their vehicles impounded until high storage fees are paid. Fines are levied on both the drivers and the owners of vehicles used for dumping.

NIMBY

To deal with the mounting solid-waste disposal problem, more landfills and resource recovery incinerators

The NIMBY syndrome is just one thing
that makes it difficult to find places to
build any type of waste-disposal facility.

are needed. But building new facilities is thwarted by another common American attitude often called the NIMBY ("Not in my backyard!") syndrome. [Everyone realizes that these facilities must be built, but no one wants to live near one.] Homeowners worry about the constant presence of trash trucks on their streets, and the real or imagined possibilities of garbage odors or other unpleasant by-products of garbage near them. They worry about their water or air being polluted or that the property values of their homes will plunge as soon as a landfill or an incinerator is built. Although in many instances their complaints are justified, they do nothing to solve the problem of what to do with the growing accumulation of solid waste.

THE NEED FOR ACTION

The problem of disposing of solid waste has been around since the cavemen and women first started dumping bones and other unwanted items in their rubbish piles, called "kitchen middens" by archeologists. [The problem is not likely to go away as long as there are people on earth to generate trash.]

Solid-waste management has become a critical problem for many areas, but improvements are being made. More states are emphasizing recycling as a way to cut down on the waste stream. Safer landfills and incinerators are being designed. Managers of solid waste are realizing that whatever methods are used, our environment must be kept free from pollution and raw materials and energy must be conserved. [These goals can be reached by recycling reusable materials, recovering maximum energy from the combustible portion of solid waste, and disposing of the residue in a way that will cause little or no harm to the environment.]

2

COLLECTING AND TRANSPORTING SOLID WASTE

No matter where solid waste ends up, it is usually far from the spot where it was first thrown away. Picking up the trash and hauling it to its final destination is an important and expensive part of waste disposal. Sometimes this means a trip of only a mile or so to a landfill on the outskirts of town. Other times it involves lengthy travel to another city, state, or even country. Waste that may begin its journey in a sanitation truck may end up being transferred to larger trucks, trains, barges, or ships for long-distance travel.

More money is spent collecting and transporting solid waste than is spent disposing of it. This is due mainly to labor costs. A lot more people are needed to collect the trash than are needed to get rid of it. As pay scales rise and the volume of solid waste increases, total collection costs climb proportionately. Transportation costs are also rising due to higher fuel prices and the longer distances traveled to reach disposal facilities. About 80 percent of a city's waste management costs go into collection and transportation.

TRASH COLLECTORS

The backbone of solid-waste management is the trash collector, who may go by a number of other titles, including garbage man or sanitation worker. Those who doubt the importance of this job should try to picture how their neighborhood would look buried under a few tons of smelly garbage. These men and women routinely fan out across the city, picking up trash and whisking it out of sight—and usually out of mind.

At one time the term "trash men" referred to recyclers. They would go through the piles of trash that had been thrown out and collect the items that still had some value. They made a profit by selling what they collected and at the same time helped keep their city clean. But as the character and amount of solid waste changed, new methods of dealing with it had to be created. Although some trash collectors still may find a few valuable items on their routes, most of the waste today is compacted inside trucks, making it difficult to sort anything out.

Most people don't realize the danger involved in a trash collector's job. A study done in New York found that next to tree-topping, collecting waste was the most hazardous occupation in the nation. Collectors are plagued with cardiovascular (heart) problems, muscle and tendon damage, arthritis, and skin infections, all related to their work. The hazards involved in lifting tons of material each day and stepping on or off of refuse trucks can result in back injuries, hernias, and accidental amputations in the truck's equipment.

Improved technology and procedures can make things easier for trash collectors. Some cities have banned trash cans and will only allow garbage bags to be set out on the curb. Using bags has been shown to speed up garbage collection because it eliminates the added motions of removing lids and returning the cans to the curb. Although this may not seem like much, when repeated hundreds of times a day it can add up. Some cities have found that crews can complete their routes in almost half the time, allowing more work to be done by fewer workers. The bags also cut down on injuries, especially back injuries that come from lifting heavy cans. Officials in Dallas, Texas, estimate that the city has already saved up to $1 million by using plastic bags. As an added benefit, bags leave the city cleaner, with less paper being blown around landfills.

COLLECTION VEHICLES

What has four wheels and flies? A garbage truck. That riddle has brought giggles to several generations of children. It used to have some validity back in the days when garbage trucks were open in back and did indeed smell bad and attract flies. The modern sanitation trucks are quite an improvement over the odorous vehicles of yesteryear. The large compactor trucks that most solid-waste collectors use today are totally closed. This not only eliminates the sight and most of the smell of garbage, it also keeps loose papers from blowing off the truck to litter the streets. Another important feature of the sanitation truck is the hydraulic arm that squeezes, or compacts, the garbage to about 30 percent of its curbside volume. The average truck can hold 10 tons of garbage.

Some communities are finding that the newer, more automated collection vehicles can save a lot in labor costs. One type of truck can pick up uniformly sized containers and automatically dump them. Since only a driver is needed, there are fewer workers that have to be paid wages, maintenance, worker's compensation time, and benefits. These trucks are also better for the workers. Lifting an overloaded can may cause injury and back pain. But an automated arm doesn't get tired, so it can work faster without accidents or injuries.

Although the automated trucks are more expensive, they can save cities money by allowing them to collect

*Modern trucks use hydraulic arms to lift
and empty heavy dumpsters.*

more trash using fewer people. Before Albany, Georgia, switched to the automated trucks, 350 to 450 houses per man were covered during one shift. With automation that number increased to between 800 and 900 houses. Some automated trucks can collect from 1,200 to 1,400 houses during one shift.

In most cities, trash is picked up from curbs or from dumpsters and driven directly to the landfill or other disposal site. But other cities may have to go through more elaborate methods to get their trash to its final destination. In New York City, most trucks carry the trash to covered piers (transfer stations), where it is loaded onto barges for a trip to the Fresh Kills landfill on Staten Island. On the Island, giant steel jaws hanging from cranes take huge bites of garbage from the barges and drop them into wagons. Tractors pull the wagons to the active dumping area.

TRANSFER STATIONS

Transporting the collected solid waste to its final destination, such as a landfill or an incinerator, can be quite costly. Either because of a lack of space or because of public opposition, new landfills are being placed further away from cities. Driving long distances not only raises fuel costs, it also raises labor costs because trash crews must spend more time driving, leaving them less time for collecting the trash. If the collectors didn't have to drive so far to unload their trucks, they could make more trips per day for less money. The solution for some areas is a transfer station.

A transfer station is a place where waste from smaller collection trucks is transferred to larger vehicles for more efficient long-distance hauling. This allows the standard collection trucks to spend their time more efficiently by picking up more trash.

The idea of using transfer stations is not new. Back in the days when garbage was collected by horse and cart, the garbage was taken to a central location. But when motorized vehicles were invented, it was easier to take the trash right to the disposal site. But now that landfills and incinerators are often very far away, transfer stations are coming back in style.

There are three types of transfer stations. In *pit stations,* the trash is dumped into pits, then pushed into an open-top transfer trailer. Some compaction of the waste results from the tractor pushing the waste into the truck.

In *direct dump stations,* the collection vehicles dump the trash right into the larger trailers. Very large trailers are needed because the waste is not compacted. Direct dumps are efficient because no intermediate handling is necessary.

The most elaborate transfer stations are the *compaction stations.* Here the waste is compacted by some means before it is loaded into the transfer trailers. Some transfer stations have the equipment to compact the waste into bales or blocks. This reduces the density of the waste by about 60 percent. Compacting wastes into bales increases the amount that can be loaded onto trucks, trains, or barges for transport to the disposal site. Bales are also easier to pack into landfills.

SHIPPING LONG DISTANCES

Some large cities, especially those in the crowded northeast section of the United States, have little or no landfill space left. They must ship their refuse long distances at tremendous expense. It is estimated that disposal costs increase by 50 cents to one dollar for *every mile* each ton of garbage is transported.

In New Jersey, half of all household waste is now trucked to out-of-state landfills up to 500 miles (800 m) away. The problem is even worse in Philadelphia. The city tried to be more progressive thirty years ago by abandoning its landfills and building incinerators. However, all but two of their incinerators have been closed because they could not meet clean-air standards. Now, both the ash from the two incinerators and the unburned trash must be taken away by truck or barge. Since 1981, when many of the landfills near Philadelphia were closed, the city's disposal costs have more than quadrupled.

Shipping garbage out-of-state is not only expensive, it is also unpopular with some of the areas receiving the shipped refuse. The South is taking action to discourage the invasion of "Yankee garbage." South Carolina now prohibits hazardous wastes from thirty-two states and Puerto Rico from being dumped within its borders.

Some wastes, especially the hazardous types, are being shipped to developing countries. These countries resent being used as dumping grounds for industrialized nations. In March 1988, officials of the west African nation of Guinea found 15,000 tons of material on an island near the capital. At first no one could figure out why the trees and plants around an abandoned quarry containing the material were dying. A government investigation found that the so-called "building material" was actually highly toxic incinerator ash from Philadelphia. A Norwegian company had shipped the waste from there and dumped it onto the island.

Other African states have also found themselves on the receiving end of toxic waste from the United States and other countries. Shippers were dumping the wastes for fees as low as $3 a ton. Some of these nations are cracking down on unauthorized dumping. Nigeria is bringing some of its citizens to trial for allowing the dumping of hazardous wastes from Italy. If they are convicted, they could be executed.

The problem is now receiving international attention. In March 1989, over a hundred countries unanimously adopted a treaty restricting shipments of hazardous waste across borders.

RAIL AND WATER TRANSPORT

For lengthy hauls, refuse can sometimes be sent by rail, or on canals or rivers. Trains and barges are able to haul much larger loads of refuse than trucks can. This could reduce the cost for long-distance hauling. It also alleviates the problems of road traffic.

One disadvantage to rail or water transportation is that, in most cases, a second transfer point is required at the disposal end. In those cases where the rail, road, or canal leads right to the so-called tipping site, a simple arrangement using dump trucks could be used. But if the tipping site is a long way from the transfer point, the cost of the third leg of transport could be very high. These methods would only be practical over very long distances. In other cases, road transport would be more economical.

Solid waste can travel many miles, from the kitchen wastebasket where it is first thrown away to its final destination at a landfill or an incinerator. The technology for transporting waste is adequate for the job that needs to be done. The real problem facing our throw-away society is not how the trash will be collected and transported, but whether or not there will be someplace to take it.

3
FROM DUMPS TO SANITARY LANDFILLS

Throughout history, the main means of disposing of solid waste has been to dump it on land. During the Middle Ages, trash and garbage were thrown out onto unpaved streets or vacant spaces. Everything from garbage to human wastes in chamber pots was tossed out the windows, often landing on unsuspecting passersby. The trash-laden streets became breeding grounds for diseases that were carried by insects and by rodents, especially rats. These unsanitary methods of waste disposal led to the outbreak of bubonic plague, including the "Black Death" epidemic of the fourteenth century that killed over a quarter of the population of Europe.

It was not until the mid-nineteenth century that it became apparent that the rotting garbage in the streets was making people sick. Then the practice of carting the trash off to the city dump became popular. At first dumps were widely used because sites were easy to find and the costs involved were relatively low. Since most household waste at that time was biodegradable, it could be handled by this method better than today's refuse can.

Although dumps outside the city were an improvement, they were still fraught with problems. The garbage attracted insects, rats, birds, and other carriers of disease. In addition, the dumps were ugly, smelled bad, and lowered the value of nearby property. In an attempt to cut down on the spread of disease, the rubbish was often burned, polluting the air with its foul-smelling smoke.

Burning trash at dumps was dangerous as well as unpleasant to those who lived nearby. One February afternoon in 1968, seven-year-old Kevin followed his older and quicker friends to the Kenilworth Dump in the District of Columbia. It was standard procedure at the dump for fires to be lit at four o'clock every afternoon to burn the large amount of garbage and trash deposited there during the day. Although the boys knew to stay out of the way, they didn't count on the shift in the wind. Flames raced across the field of papers and other trash, swirling out of control. Kevin was cut off from his friends. They managed to get away, but Kevin died in the deadly flames.

SANITARY LANDFILLS

Over the past half century, communities have become more conscious of the effects of open dumping on the environment. These dumps cause problems with smoke pollution, odors, disease-spreading pests, and the contamination of ground and surface water. From these concerns, the practice of using sanitary landfills came into being.

In a sanitary landfill, each day's waste is compacted by heavy machinery, then covered with about 6 inches (15 cm) of dirt. This layer of dirt reduces the foul odors drifting to nearby areas and holds down the lightweight paper and plastic litter that would otherwise blow away. Sanitary landfills are also not as attractive to rats, birds, and other disease-carrying pests. Since the garbage and

30

*In spite of efforts to confine trash disposal
to sanitary landfills, people continue
to dump items where they are not wanted.*

the top layer of soil are compacted every day, it is difficult for rats to establish a stable network of tunnels and dens in which to hide and reproduce. The soil also reduces the amount of water that seeps through the refuse, contaminating nearby ground or surface water.

The dirt used to cover the daily accumulation of trash is either dug out of trenches in the landfill or brought in from a nearby excavation. Some communities can get it from highway departments or building contractors. Florida's Sarasota County agreed to dig several lakes ranging from ten to fifty acres in size for a housing development. More than a million cubic yards of soil were excavated and taken to the landfill to be used as cover. This was enough to extend the life of the Bee Ridge landfill another fifteen years.

In spite of the advantages of sanitary landfills, open dumps can still be found all over the United States. This is primarily because direct dumping is a much cheaper way to get rid of solid waste than maintaining a landfill at recommended standards.

TYPES OF LANDFILLS

Landfills are versatile in that they fit into a variety of topographies. The waste can be deposited on flat or gently rolling land, or put into trenches, quarries, pits, or other indentations. The *trench method* is used when the ground water is low and the soil is more than 6 feet (1.8 m) deep. It is best suited for flat or gently rolling land. In some cases, the dirt used for the cover is excavated from the area just ahead of the present dumping site. The dirt dug out of the trench is then used immediately to cover the newly dumped trash behind it. In this way, the dirt only has to be handled once. In other landfills, a trench is excavated and refuse is emptied into it and compacted. The dirt used to cover it is taken from the excavation of an adjoining trench. By the time one trench is filled, the next trench is ready for use.

The *area method* can conform to most topographies and is often used when large quantities of solid waste are being deposited. When the site is relatively flat, the solid waste is deposited and compacted to form a slope rising above the natural ground level. In the area method, low-lying areas such as ravines, swampy places, and eroded sections are filled up.

Although landfills may be quite large, only a small area, called a *cell,* is filled at a time. When one cell is filled, compacted, and covered, then dumping is begun in the next cell. The cell is usually square, with sides sloped as steeply as possible. Sloping the sides about 30 degrees keeps the amount of cover material needed at a minimum and provides good compaction of waste, particularly when spread in layers about 2 feet (61 cm) thick.

FRESH KILLS

Sanitary landfills may be an improvement over open dumps, but they are not necessarily pleasant places. New York City's landfill is a good example. The city's five boroughs generate more waste than any other city in the nation—an estimated 27,750 tons each day in 1986. Up to 17,000 tons of that garbage is dumped each day into the world's largest landfill, a facility on the edge of Staten Island with the ironic name of "Fresh Kills." (The word "kill" comes from the Dutch word for "channel.")

Fresh Kills is an environmental nightmare. It attracts sea gulls, generates foul odors, and contaminates the water. Its two peaks of garbage reached the height of 150 feet (46 m) in 1987. At the present rate of growth, by the year 2000, Fresh Kills could tower 500 feet (152 m) above the New York harbor. It will be the highest point on the eastern seaboard south of Maine.

But as unpleasant as Fresh Kills is, New York City cannot afford to close the 3,000-acre, 40-year-old dump. It has already had to close most of its landfills, leaving only Fresh Kills and one other, small landfill to handle its waste. If Fresh Kills were to close tomorrow, New York City would have to do what many of its neighboring communities do—ship its 8 million tons of waste to Ohio at $120 a ton. That would cost the city a staggering $1 billion a year. So for the time being, at least, Fresh Kills will remain an odorous symbol of urban civilization.

DWINDLING NUMBERS

The biggest problem with landfills is that there are not enough of them. At a time when our waste stream is growing due to population increases and the accelerated rate at which we throw things away, our landfills are decreasing in numbers. The statistics are alarming. From 1978 to 1988, an estimated 70 percent of the landfill sites closed. Another 1,200 are scheduled to close between 1989 and 1994, although some may be allowed to stay open longer if alternatives cannot be found. By 1995 the landfills in more than half the cities in the United States are expected to run out of room.

Landfill closures would not be a problem if new ones were opening up at the same rate, but this is not the case. Between 1981 and 1986 only 563 new landfills were opened—a 35 percent decrease from the five-year period a decade earlier. This means that greater amounts of waste must be hauled to fewer landfills, making them fill up even faster.

Disposal sites have become so scarce in some areas

that haulers are crossing state lines in increasing numbers, searching for a place to dump their loads. To prevent this practice, which has become a way of life in New England, a number of states in the region have passed laws that ban out-of-state wastes. Some illegal haulers still try to sneak garbage over state lines.

Opening new landfills is becoming increasingly difficult. One reason is the lack of suitable land. Ideally, landfill sites would be close to the cities and communities they serve. This cuts down on the high cost of transporting refuse to distant sites. But in most cities, especially in the Northeast, land near the cities is at a premium. Communities can't afford to pay the high prices for the land. And then there is the even bigger problem, especially near communities where sites are most needed, of the NIMBY syndrome.

Citizen groups opposing landfills are sometimes justified in their complaints against landfill sites and sometimes not. The biggest problems come from those groups who become almost violent in their opposition without really looking at the facts. They offer no solutions or alternatives. Many don't understand how critical the problem is. They don't consider the problem urgent as long as their trash is being picked up regularly and hauled out of sight.

Stricter regulations by the Environmental Protection Agency (EPA) that are designed to make landfills safer are also making it harder for new ones to open. These regulations require landfills to monitor hazardous waste and methane gas; to keep harmful wastes from discharging into water supplies; and to control rodents, insects, fire, and odor. Although the new standards are reasonable, few of today's municipal dumps could meet them. When the limitations take full effect in 1991, some landfills may be forced to close while some new ones will probably not open. The EPA estimates that its landfill regulations will eventually add $800 to $900 million a year to the nation's garbage disposal costs, which already are costing some $4 to $5 billion annually. This will put a tremendous financial strain on the states and localities that must pay for these added expenses.

BIODEGRADABLE VS. NONBIODEGRADABLE WASTE

Nearly every day, in every city or town across the country, sanitation trucks rumble over the streets making their rounds. But once the cans have been emptied or the dumpsters unloaded, what happens to all that trash?

At the landfill, sanitation workers dump their loads into the area of the landfill presently being filled. Although the trash was compacted in the trucks, it is further compacted by bulldozers or heavy compactor machines that spread out the waste as they pack it down. In one day the layer of compacted trash rises an average of 8 feet (2.5 m). At the end of the day, the waste is covered with a 6-inch (15-cm) layer of earth.

Once the garbage is covered with dirt, the biodegradable items, such as food wastes, paper, grass cuttings, and other yard wastes, begin to decay. At first, microorganisms called *aerobes* that are present in the covering of dirt use the oxygen in the dirt to begin decomposing the biodegradable items. This chemical reaction causes the temperature within the landfill to rise. The heat kills much of the disease-causing bacteria. After the oxygen is used up, other microorganisms, called *anaerobes*, which live in the absence of oxygen, continue to feed on the refuse. During this process several gases are given off, including methane, carbon dioxide, ammonia, and hydrogen sulfide. The refuse continues to decompose for many years.

Other wastes, such as glass, plastic, aluminum, and

other metals, are nonbiodegradable. They clog our landfills because they do not decay. Today, these nonbiodegradable items make up a larger portion of the waste stream than they did in the past.

An effort is being made to turn some nonbiodegradable products into biodegradable ones. One example of this is plastic, which is difficult to burn or recycle and can stay in landfills forever. Plastics are formed by long chains of molecules called *polymers*. These chains are wound so tightly that microbes can't get at them to break them down. Now, cornstarch can be mixed with the plastic to separate the polymer chains. When bacteria eat the cornstarch, the plastic falls apart into pieces that can be ingested by the microorganisms.

Early attempts at making biodegradable plastics were not very successful. Some could only disintegrate in sunlight, which is unavailable at the bottom of a landfill. Others fell apart when they came in contact with water. These could be a nightmare for those carrying home a plastic shopping bag containing a leaky milk bottle. The market for biodegradable plastic products is small now, but as more environmentally concerned governments place restrictions on plastics in their landfills, the market should grow.

One product causing major problems for landfills is the disposable diaper. About 16 billion disposable diapers find their way to landfills each year. That's enough to blanket twenty-five football fields with piles of diapers reaching thirty stories high. There are a lot of things more dangerous than diapers in landfills, but they are still a problem. Although 60 percent of the diaper is made of wood pulp and fluff that could decompose, it is enclosed in plastic that can keep it intact indefinitely. Not only are diapers a problem because of the tremendous number being thrown away, but they may also carry diseases such as intestinal viruses that cause polio, hepatitis, and meningitis. If they get into the ground water they could contaminate the water supply. So far, this has not happened as far as anyone can tell. However, some states are not waiting to see if it will. Nebraska plans to ban the sale of nonbiodegradable diapers beginning in 1993.

A more serious problem today is the number of toxic chemicals that are found in landfills. Although most industrial waste containing toxic chemicals is banned from landfills, the number of chemicals found in normal household trash is enough to be threatening. Without realizing the danger, people throw away things such as cleaning fluids, pesticides, paint thinners, batteries, and battery acids, which could send toxic chemicals into the water, soil, or air.

DANGEROUS BY-PRODUCTS

There are two unwanted by-products in landfills. One is *leachate,* a poisonous "stew" of chemicals that can leak into the groundwater. The other is methane gas, which can be explosive under certain conditions.

When rainwater or melted snow passes through solid waste in landfills, it can pick up finely suspended soil matter, microbial waste products, dissolved materials, and even toxic or poisonous chemicals. The result is leachate, a solution that may contain highly concentrated pollutants. This leachate can be dangerous to humans when it seeps out of dumps into groundwater. It can be carried by underground streams or rainwater to wells or reservoirs, where it can contaminate drinking water. This is especially true with landfills in wetlands, on flood plains, or over aquifers, the channels through which groundwater flows.

In a 1980 study the EPA found that 90 percent of the landfills in the eastern United States leak toxic substances into groundwater. The Fresh Kills landfill discharges an estimated 1 million gallons (15 million l) of toxic leachate every day. The problem with leachate is not as great in the arid West because there is not as much precipitation there.

Another dangerous by-product of landfills is methane, one of the gases produced by rotting garbage. Much of municipal solid waste is made up of carbon, oxygen, and hydrogen with smaller amounts of nitrogen and sulfur. As the waste decomposes, gases are given off. The mixture is from 50 to 60 percent methane, a colorless and explosive gas that is also the main ingredient in natural gas used for cooking, heating, and generating electricity. In addition to methane, landfill gas contains 40 to 50 percent carbon dioxide, with traces of ammonia and hydrogen sulfide.

If methane production is not controlled at a landfill, the gas can migrate underground away from the area. When methane moves into the soil it can kill nearby vegetation by eliminating oxygen from the root zone.

When methane reaches concentrations of 5 to 15 percent, it can be explosive. This can happen if the methane seeps into closed structures, such as sewer lines or buildings. In 1983 a town house located across the street from a closed landfill in Madison, Wisconsin, exploded when methane seeped into the building. Two tenants were burned in the explosion. Since then, a methane-control system has been installed at the landfill.

In the fall of 1985 nearly explosive levels of methane were found in the basements of several homes near the Midway Landfill in a suburb of Seattle, Washington. Eleven families had to be evacuated. The city ended up buying two hundred homes that were threatened by the gas. Midway Landfill is now being cleaned up.

The production of methane gas can be a problem at landfills, but it can also be an asset. Gas-recovery systems have been developed to collect landfill gas for use in boilers or in turbines to generate electricity. When most of the water vapor and carbon dioxide are removed from the gas, the remaining methane can be pumped directly into natural gas utility pipelines.

The landfills that produce the most gas are those where plenty of organic matter has been dumped. The landfill must be deep and large, containing at least a million tons of refuse, in order to produce a substantial amount of gas. With this requirement, it is not surprising that the world's largest methane recovery facility is at Fresh Kills. Through its one hundred wells spread over 400 acres of the landfill, the plant is capable of producing almost 10 million cubic feet per day of raw landfill gas. The gas travels through an underground collection system to a plant where it is processed to remove trace elements, carbon dioxide, and moisture. The purified gas is then sold to the Brooklyn Union Gas Company. It provides enough fuel to heat 50,000 homes. Gas supplies from this site should be plentiful for years to come because methane is produced for decades after a landfill stops receiving garbage.

MAKING LANDFILLS SAFE

Although landfills are regarded as one of the best methods for solid-waste disposal, there are certain problems that can only be avoided with proper design, construction, and operation. To increase landfill safety, the federal Resource Conservation and Recovery Act (RCRA) was passed in 1976. As a result, newly built landfills must follow strict design standards and construction procedures.

One of the major concerns is a landfill's effect on water sources. Much of the United States depends on surface water such as lakes, reservoirs, and rivers to meet its water needs. Since many communities are located

A Sanitary Landfill

New landfill technologies (top) can protect groundwater from leachate, which is pumped out of the liners that trap it. Methane leakage can be detected and burned off by a flare, but another alternative is a methane recovery system (bottom). The system collects the methane and fuels a turbine to generate electricity.

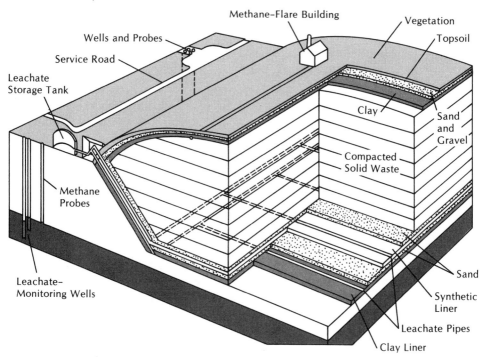

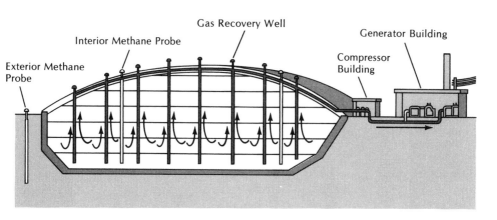

on the banks of rivers, the pollutants discharged from one community often become part of the water supply of another further downstream. Sometimes the source of these pollutants are landfills that have been improperly sited, designed, and operated. Dangerous chemicals can leave these landfills as runoff or leachate and eventually find their way into lakes, reservoirs, and rivers.

The possibility of leachate seeping into groundwater is also a danger. Groundwater exists in massive quantities under most regions of the country. Since over half the population of the United States depends on groundwater for drinking, it is critical that its quality be protected.

Groundwater flows through an aquifer that may be separated from the surface by layers of different types of soil, such as sand, silt, or clay. The type of soil the leachate has to go through determines how long it will take to reach the aquifer. The process may take months or even years. Also, since groundwater itself may move only a few feet a day, it may be years before the effect of a polluting source is detected at a distant site. By 1984 the EPA had identified over 400 sites where groundwater contamination had become serious enough to require remedial action in order to prevent a direct threat to drinking water sources.

In order to protect groundwater, plastic or clay liners can be placed at the foundation of the landfill to trap the leachate. These must be installed correctly so that no punctures or tears occur during installation or when garbage is first dumped into the landfill. This normally requires placing layers of sand above and below the liner for added protection. If this is not done, it is possible for some of the leachate to leak out through pinholes or seams.

In some areas clay is used as a liner. Whereas plastic is designed to trap the leachate, the objective of clay liners is to achieve a slow filtering of the leachate. As the leachate slowly percolates through the clay liner it undergoes chemical reactions that reduce the concentration of contaminants. In some circumstances, clay liners may be more effective than plastic liners.

The type of liner used depends partly on what is available. Where clay is abundant and relatively inexpensive, clay liners may be preferred. Plastic liners may be better in areas where clay liners might leak leachate slowly and continuously into water sources. In some areas a combination of the two is used. When clay liners are used, the liner must be installed in a way that will keep it moist at all times so that it will not crack.

Liners create a "tub" that collects rainwater containing leachate. Landfills must have a means of treating this water before it can be released into the environment. Some leachate may have to be collected and disposed of as an industrial hazardous waste. Most landfill leachate is sent directly to a sewage-treatment plant, but not all plants are capable of handling the highly contaminated water. In these cases, the leachate must be treated on site before being shipped to the sewage-treatment plant.

Reducing the amount of water that is allowed to seep through a landfill can help control the leachate problem. Some of the newer landfills are built with a cover of soil or synthetic material that diverts the rain or snow away from the waste. Vegetation grown on top of the landfill can also help minimize erosion and use up some of the water instead of letting it flow into the landfill.

Choosing a good site for a landfill is also important. It must be a safe distance from streams, wells, and other water sources. The landfill should not be placed in floodplains or above fractured bedrock that would provide an easy flow path for the leachate to get to water sources. Areas of low rainfall and high evaporation are best.

Even when precautions have been taken, it is still possible for leachate to leak out of a landfill. Therefore, monitoring devices need to be installed in order to detect leaks. This can be done by using a series of observation wells and sampling stations. By comparing water quality upstream and downstream from a landfill, it is possible to detect any form of contamination.

In addition to controlling leachate, landfills must make some provisions for controlling the buildup of methane and other gases produced by the decomposing garbage. In some cases vents can be installed through the top cover to allow the methane to escape. It can often be burned off with flares. It is important that these vents be kept away from buildings or other enclosures where the concentration of gas could reach explosive levels.

Birds that flock around landfills to feast on fresh garbage can also be a safety hazard, especially if there are airports nearby. Since both airports and landfills need a lot of space, they are often located near each other on the outskirts of a city. They also have in common the fact that they both attract things that fly—sometimes into one another. In October 1960, a turbo-prop plane crashed at Boston's Logan Airport. Inspectors believe that the crash was the direct result of the plane flying through a flock of starlings. Sixty-two passengers lost their lives in this tragic event. Whenever these two types of facilities must be located in the same area, special precautions should be taken to discourage the feeding of birds.

SEATTLE'S SUCCESS STORY

Seattle has one of the best and safest dumps in the nation. Each day, 1,450 tons of solid waste are brought to Cedar Hills, a 900-acre landfill 30 miles (48 km) south of the city. Here the trash is pulverized by giant compactors with hobnailed wheels, then smoothed flat by bulldozers. At the end of each day the exposed trash is covered with at least 6 inches (15 cm) of earth. A 1,000-foot (300-m) buffer zone separates the landfill from the surrounding community. The trash is dumped into pits that have been lined with layers of sand, plastic, and bentonite, an absorbent clay mineral. These waterproof liners protect the groundwater. A network of tubing collects leachate, and plastic pipes crisscross the landfill to siphon off methane gas to nearby burners. A lattice of fishing lines is suspended over every pit to discourage the thousands of sea gulls and other birds in the area.

FROM DUMPS TO PARKS

Closing a landfill is more complicated than just adding an extra layer or two of dirt and walking away from it. Provisions must be made to ensure that the evils lurking beneath the dirt will not haunt future generations. New state and federal regulations that govern landfill closures went into effect in the early 1980s. Generally, they require a landfill owner or operator to close the landfill in a way that will minimize threats to human health and to the environment. Among other things, landfill sites must be equipped with devices to monitor groundwater and air emissions. But closing a landfill properly, especially an old one that didn't have to follow many regulations when it was being built, can easily run into millions of dollars, depending on the size and condition of the site. Management understandably tends to drag its feet when it comes to satisfying costly regulations.

Once the last bit of refuse has been squeezed into a landfill, the area can be put to good use. Closed landfills can be made into parks and recreation areas with running tracks, ball fields, picnic grounds, golf courses, tennis courts, and even ski slopes. Turning landfills into parks and other recreation areas not only saves cities the cost of acquiring land, which is not always even available, but also converts an eyesore into an attractive and functional area.

Mt. Trashmore in Virginia Beach, Virginia, has been turned into a beautiful recreation area, providing activities for thousands of residents. The Riverview Highlands Ski Resort south of Detroit, Michigan, was also once a solid-waste disposal site. Now it has eight slopes, several lifts, and a vertical drop of 150 feet (46 m). With the addition of more solid waste, an expert slope with a vertical drop of 176 feet (54 m) is planned. Although this is not high by Rocky Mountain standards, it makes an impressive hill in the flat terrain of southeastern Michigan.

Turning landfills into recreational areas takes as much planning as building the landfill in the first place. As the garbage settles in a landfill, the ground can shift. The amount of settlement will depend on the type of waste that has been put into the landfill and how deep the landfill is. Deeper landfills settle more. Although most of the settling takes place in the first three years or so, less dramatic settlement continues for many years. It may even be necessary to add another layer of refuse after two or three years.

Because the settling can be damaging, major buildings or paved surfaces, including tennis and basketball courts, should not be constructed directly on top of the fill areas. If buildings are to be constructed in this area, they need to be secured with pilings driven into the ground at very high pressures and compaction, making the structure almost an island.

Planting trees on top of a landfill can be a problem unless it has been covered with an impermeable cap that would keep gas from getting into the soil. Tree roots can penetrate the cap and become exposed to the methane gas collecting in the landfill. The trees usually die when methane gas suffocates their roots.

Another worry about closed landfills is not knowing what sorts of hazardous wastes may appear years later. Before the 1976 RCRA, a lot of hazardous waste was dumped into landfills along with municipal solid waste. Special care and monitoring must be included in closure plans to make sure no hazardous substances find their way out of the landfill and cause health problems for the people using the area. This step makes the transformation of such sites into parks more difficult and expensive.

STILL ROOM FOR IMPROVEMENT

In spite of new regulations and improved technology, most of today's landfills are still below standard. The technology to control leachate and gaseous emissions from landfills has not been implemented in most sites currently under operation. Of the 6,000 municipal solid-waste landfills, 15 percent are lined, fewer than 5 percent collect leachate, and 25 percent monitor groundwater. About a hundred landfills have methane-collection projects used for resource recovery and energy production.

Continued efforts must be made to build safer landfills because they will always be necessary. Even with recycling and the increased use of incinerators at resource recovery facilities, landfills will still be necessary, if for no other reason than to accept the residues from other treatment processes.

4

INCINERATION AND RESOURCE RECOVERY

The idea of burning trash has been around ever since people discovered that they could keep their fires going by fueling them with items they had previously thrown away. People in medieval days found a way to have incinerators come to them. A horse-drawn wagon that was coated with clay to protect it from fire was pulled through the streets. Townspeople could throw their garbage into the portable bonfire.

Since the late nineteenth century, incinerators have been the most common method of waste disposal for European countries. Their population densities have made it difficult for them to find large areas of land to use as landfills. As a result, they got a head start on developing the incinerator technology.

When the United States tried to adopt European technology to its own incineration plants the results were less than successful. One problem is that Americans have different types of trash than Europeans. Refuse in the United States is full of plastics, which produce high temperatures and corrosive gases. Also, Americans tend to throw away everything from refrigerators to steel-belted tires, whereas the Europeans are more likely to reuse or recycle more of their refuse.

49

Although dumps and landfills have always been the primary means of waste disposal in the United States, incineration has been used in the past. During the two world wars, when energy was scarce, incinerators were used to produce electricity. But in the affluence that followed World War II, not much effort was made to continue this practice.

The early incinerators spewed plumes of ugly black smoke into the air. Enough people became concerned about what this was doing to air quality that the government finally took action. The Clean Air Act passed in 1970 required air pollution controls at incinerators. But most communities didn't want to pay for these expensive modifications, so they went back to using landfills, a cheaper method of waste disposal. There was almost a total abandonment of incineration for a while.

Later in the 1970s, the general consensus was that new methods of disposing of waste other than landfilling had to be developed. The then newly formed Environmental Protection Agency funded a number of research projects in order to develop state-of-the-art technology for solid-waste disposal. Most of these projects involved building resource recovery or "waste-to-energy" facilities in which the burning of waste was used to produce steam for heating or for generating electricity. Researchers on these projects didn't pay much attention to the systems operating in Europe. It was assumed that since those systems had been developed much earlier, they wouldn't be of much help in designing systems for the future.

Millions of dollars were assigned by the EPA for research and development. Experimental resource recovery systems were built in several American cities, but most of them were essentially failures. Unfortunately, their flaws didn't become apparent until after large sums of money had been spent for construction and operation. Their problems can be attributed to a lack of ongoing, solid research in the years before and a desire to find quick solutions. This caused some cities to adopt unproven technologies that were inferior to the European systems that had been in use for decades. For example, by 1979, Switzerland, Sweden, and West Germany were each processing over 50 percent of their municipal solid waste in resource recovery incinerators compared to less than 2 percent in the United States. Today, our resource recovery facilities use much of the technology developed in Europe.

RESOURCE RECOVERY

The average American citizen throws out nearly a ton of solid waste each year. If this ton of waste is taken to a landfill, it does little more than take up space. But if it is processed in a resource recovery facility, that same ton of waste could produce about 500 kilowatt hours of electric power, roughly the same output as the burning of one barrel of oil. In addition, the 500 pounds (227 kg) of residue left after incineration could provide 125 pounds (57 kg) of ferrous scrap material and 325 pounds (159 kg) of material that could be used in building roads. Ideally, out of 1 ton, only 50 pounds (23 kg) would need to be placed in a landfill.

The modern resource recovery or waste-to-energy plants are a far cry from the dirty incinerators of past generations. In most of the plants, the furnace walls are lined with water-filled pipes. The heat from the burning refuse turns the water into steam that can be piped to nearby areas to be used as heat or to drive turbines to generate electricity.

In the past, the cost involved in building these facilities has made them unpopular in most areas of the United States where landfilling was more economical. But with the country's landfill capacity rapidly shrink-

51

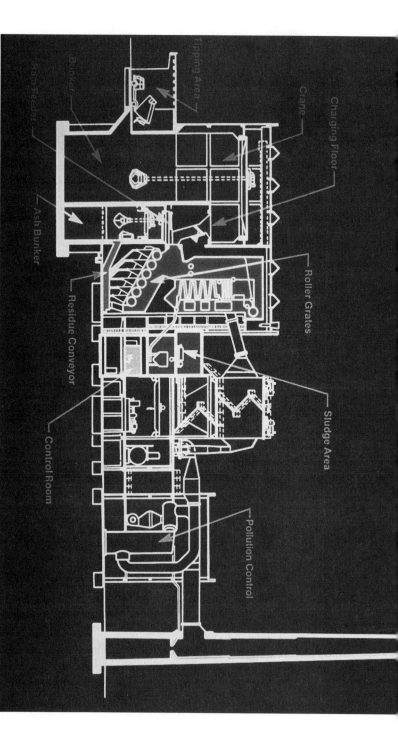

Tipping Area

Bunker

Ram Feeder

Crane

Charging Floor

Ash Bunker

Residue Conveyor

Roller Grates

Control Room

Sludge Area

Pollution Control

*Above: the Dutchess County Resource Recovery
Center in Poughkeepsie, New York, incinerates
up to four hundred tons of garbage a day to
produce nine megawatts of electricity.*

*Left: this diagram of a resource-recovery plant
shows the care that is taken to keep pollution
and other wastes from leaving the plant.*

ing, the expense involved in depositing solid waste in the remaining landfills has made building resource recovery facilities more competitive economically.

The young waste-to-energy industry in the United States got off to a slow start in the 1970s when it was plagued with breakdowns and costly mistakes. But the development of new techniques and equipment is making resource recovery a more attractive alternative. The industry started showing rapid growth in the 1980s. A 1989 survey done by the Institute of Resource Recovery showed that the total industry capacity in 1989 was 68,619 tons of waste a day. It is expected to rise to 171,025 tons of waste a day by 1993.

Plants that turn garbage into power are expensive but not necessarily out of reach. When built properly, much of the cost is offset by the revenue collected from energy sales and from tipping fees, the amount charged for each ton of trash dumped at the facility. A market for the energy produced is guaranteed by a law passed in 1978 requiring electric utilities to purchase, at a fair price, electricity offered for sale by private producers.

Most of the modern resource recovery facilities have been profitable for the leading companies that run them. However, mastering the technology has not been easy. Some communities have wound up with much bigger disposal bills than they had anticipated.

TYPES OF RESOURCE RECOVERY FACILITIES

The most common type of resource recovery plant is a "mass-burn" facility where municipal waste is dumped "as is" into the furnaces, with little or no presorting of waste. One mass-burn facility is operating in Babylon, New York. The $84 million facility is designed to burn 268,000 tons of garbage a year. Inside the facility, trucks dump their loads of waste into a giant waste pit. Twin cranes lift huge bites of trash into two hoppers leading to the furnace below. The high temperatures used to incinerate the garbage also heat a boiler that produces steam for generating electricity. Before the smoke goes out the stack it passes through two scrubber units that remove acid gas and a filter system that removes ash particles. Ash collecting at the bottom of the furnace is removed by conveyors. It comes out of the furnace in wetted-down crumbly cakes.

The other type of resource recovery facility makes refuse-derived fuel (RDF). Here, glass and metals are removed and the remaining solid waste is shredded to produce either a confettilike or pelletized fuel. This fuel can be burned in specially designed boilers or mixed in small proportions with coal. Some RDF plants also isolate organic wastes that can be composted, such as food and yard wastes. This lowers the moisture content, improving the quality of the fuel produced. As of 1988 there were thirteen refuse-derived-fuel facilities in operation in the United States with the capacity to process 3.4 million tons of waste per year.

Mass-burning plants are cheaper to build and simpler to operate than the RDF facilities. However, the mass-burning plants produce more residue ash that must be dealt with. A plant that burns 3,000 tons of solid waste a day may produce as much as 1,000 tons of ash that must be disposed of.

ADVANTAGES AND DISADVANTAGES OF INCINERATION

One advantage of incinerators is that they are space-savers. Not only do they need less space than landfills to begin with, they extend the life of existing landfills by reducing the volume of waste to be disposed of. The number of workers needed to run a resource recovery plant is relatively small. Many plants can get by with only four operators for each shift, including a crane driver, a reception attendant, a control room attendant, and a general-purpose employee. However, more skill is needed in this type of operation than is needed in landfills, so workers must be paid higher wages.

In spite of the advantages of resource recovery plants, they are not without major problems. Opponents worry most about their impact on the environment, from toxic gases being released into the atmosphere to the concentrated toxins in the ash residue that must be buried in landfills.

Originally, incinerators exhausted all their gases and particles directly into the air because it was considered too expensive to do otherwise. But the Clean Air Act of 1970 required incinerators to install pollution-control devices to remove impurities from the gases pouring out of the smokestacks. These tighter air-pollution laws are partially responsible for the increase in toxic substances found in the ash residue. The dioxin, lead, and cadmium that once went up the chimney now go down the ash chute. The toxins are just as unpopular in the ground as they were in the air.

Many operators found the cost of complying with these new regulations prohibitive and closed down their incinerators. It was not until the 1980s when the decreasing number of landfills pushed up the cost of disposing of solid waste that incineration again became economically competitive.

Air pollution can be a very real problem when incineration is done improperly. Solid waste sent to incinerators contains a diverse sampling of chemically different materials, including paper, wood, metals, glass, and plastics. When this mixture is burned, some of the materials give off certain gases. Other compounds may form through the interaction of various materials when they are burned together.

There has been some concern about the incineration of materials containing polychlorinated biphenyls (PCBs) because low concentrations of these chemicals have been shown to cause cancer in laboratory animals. Because some of the items that end up in incinerators are made of PCBs, there is the worry that these chemicals will find their way into the atmosphere. However, existing data indicate that at least 99.9 percent of the PCBs contained in municipal solid waste are destroyed by the high temperatures used in modern incinerators.

Another worry is that the incinerators will give off dioxin, a highly poisonous substance that is produced when temperatures are not high enough during the burning of certain household items such as some solvents and plastics. Studies done at municipal solid-waste incinerators indicate that by raising the combustion temperatures to at least 1,800° F (1,000° C), dioxins and furans are significantly reduced. Most of the small amounts that remain are removed from the smoke with scrubbers and filters.

PROTECTING
THE ATMOSPHERE

By law, incinerators must filter out harmful gases and particles that may pollute the air. One of the unwanted materials is *fly ash,* which is made up of fine particles of ashes, soot, and dust floating up the chimney from the burning refuse. For every ton of solid waste burned, about 25 pounds (11 kg) goes up the chimney as fly ash. Properly built incinerators catch these particles before they are allowed to escape into the atmosphere.

Fine particles can be filtered out by passing the smoke

through porous bags. Several bags are contained in units called *baghouses*. When the bags become caked with fly ash, the air flow is reversed to blow the cakes of ash off the bags. The clumps of fly ash are collected and added to the bottom ash for final disposal. Baghouses are best for smaller facilities. Large incinerators may produce too much fly ash for the bags to handle and their higher temperatures may damage the bags.

Another way to trap the fine particles in gas is with metal plates called *electrostatic precipitators*. As the fly ash is carried toward the smokestack by hot gases, the particles are given an electric charge. Then they pass between metal plates that have the opposite electric charge. The particles are attracted to the plates and stick to them in the same way that tiny pieces of paper are attracted to a comb that has been charged electrically by passing it through hair. Periodically, the particles are shaken off the plates into a bin. Electrostatic precipitators are successful at removing 95 to 99 percent of the fly ash. The tiny amounts of dioxins that may escape into the air with the gas are considered to be well within safe levels.

Besides mechanisms to filter out particles in the smoke, incinerators are also equipped with scrubbers to purify the flue gas. The scrubbers spray a wet or dry calcium compound into the smoke. The compound chemically neutralizes the acid in the gas.

BOTTOM
ASH

When solid waste is burned in an incinerator, approximately 20 to 25 percent of it remains as ash. Since toxic metals become more concentrated during burning, this ash residue may contain concentrated forms of dioxin and toxic metals such as mercury, lead, and cadmium. This is becoming more of a problem because of the increasing number of resource recovery facilities being used in the United States and also because of the more complex nature of the waste that is burned. A recent Environmental Defense Fund report found that the average concentration of lead and cadmium in ash exceeds the regulatory limit defining hazardous waste. For the time being, the EPA has exempted incinerator ash from the laws that regulate other hazardous waste, but that may change.

Because of the possibility of having toxic substances in the ash, disposing of it becomes a problem. If the ash is buried in poorly sealed landfills, the toxic chemicals have the potential of leaking into groundwater. One solution may be to require that the ash be deposited in landfills specifically designed for incinerator ash. However, ash disposal sites are expensive, costing up to $1 million per acre, and building them draws strong opposition from area residents.

The amount of ash deposited in landfills can be reduced where more creative uses can be found for it. In Europe, where incineration has been used more extensively for a much longer time, ash from incinerators has been used both as fill material and as part of road construction materials. There are other promising uses of the ash. It can be used as a landfill cover to save the cost of shipping in dirt. It can be mixed with other materials to make cement or road pavements. The State University of New York at Stony Brook, Long Island, is experimenting to see if ash made into huge cinderblocks will leak toxins if used to make artificial underwater reefs. Before any widespread use of incinerator ash can be made, more research is needed to make sure that its use does not introduce hazardous materials into the environment through the air, ground, or water.

ACCEPTANCE IS SLOW

Like any other form of solid-waste disposal, resource recovery facilities often meet with opposition. As with landfills, the chief obstacle is the NIMBY syndrome. The concerns of the residents are much the same—threats of potential air and water pollution, increased traffic from sanitation trucks, and plunging property values. In Philadelphia, which has one of the worst trash-disposal problems in the nation, citizens have battled against an incinerator since 1981 even though their disposal and landfill costs have skyrocketed by 270 percent. New York's former mayor, Edward I. Koch, tried since 1984 to build incinerators in all five boroughs of New York to cope with over 27,000 tons of trash generated each day. As his term came to a close at the end of 1989, he still was not able to start production on even one of these incinerators because of a series of court battles and environmental impact reviews.

Opposition to resource recovery plants has been subsiding in many areas as the new plants prove themselves. Modern facilities are generally attractive and safe. High-temperature burning—as hot as 2,800°F (1,540°C)—and computer-controlled feeders that keep the combustion constant even as garbage flow varies, have cut pollution. Present-day antipollution devices can reduce toxic emissions by as much as 99 percent.

Some of the fears faced by NIMBY supporters have not materialized. When run properly, resource recovery facilities do not have problems with odors, litter, or water pollution. The interior of the plant is kept at a lower level of air pressure than the outside air, so that no air from the garbage pit escapes to the outside. The only air coming out of the plant is through the flue gas, and that is odorless. Since the trucks are unloaded inside a closed building, there is no problem of litter blowing around the outside. And there is little or no waste water coming out of the modern facilities so there is no significant environmental impact on either surface or groundwater supplies.

The NIMBY syndrome is not the only thing keeping new resource recovery facilities from being built. In some communities there is opposition from the recycling industry, which wants its share of the municipal solid waste. In the United States there are roughly 1,500 wastepaper dealers who supply more than 200 paper and paperboard mills. These dealers rely entirely on wastepaper for their raw material. But since newspapers, cardboard, and other paper products make up half of all residential solid waste, eliminating them from the waste stream cuts heavily into the amount of fuel needed by the resource recovery facilities. In Akron, Ohio, the city government passed a "flow-control" law to make sure it had enough solid waste to supply its waste-to-energy plant. It laid claim to all solid waste as soon as it was discarded within the city limits. In effect, it outlawed recycling.

In some ways, the recycling and waste-to-energy industries can be compatible. Removing some incombustible materials, such as metals and glass, can actually improve the quality of the fuel and decrease the wear and tear on furnaces.

Another complaint against waste-to-energy plants is that they may increase the demand for wood pulp. This would result in more trees being cut down and used just once for paper, which would then be burned for energy.

When considering various waste-disposal methods, it is important for city leaders to consider the needs of both the resource recovery and recycling industries. If proper planning is neglected, an aggressive paper-recycling program could reduce the supply of fuel to a resource recovery facility designed for a certain volume of waste. The plant could lose more in revenue from its

61

declining energy production that it could earn by recycling some of the waste.

SUCCESS STORY

One successful resource recovery plant in Saugus, Massachusetts, has been operating since 1973. It receives
solid waste from parts of Boston and sixteen suburban
communities. Truckloads of solid waste are weighed,
then dumped into a large storage pit. Overhead cranes
scoop up mouthfuls of waste and deposit them into the
hopper that feeds the furnace. Inside the furnace, the
waste burns on top of a series of grates that jerk fre-
quently to keep the burning mass moving downward.
In the boiler's 60-foot (18-m) walls and ceiling are a
mass of steel tubes filled with water. The heat turns the
water into steam, which is piped to a General Electric
plant less than a mile away. Gases produced by the
burning waste pass through devices specially designed
to control air emissions. Large magnets remove scrap
iron from the ash.

TO BURN OR NOT TO BURN

Resource recovery is not the right choice for every
community. The facilities are extremely expensive,
costing in the tens or hundreds of millions of dollars.
Many communities can't afford them. Also, the plants
take from three to five years to construct, so they do
not offer an immediate solution. The community must
also make sure it has a need for the supply of energy
produced at the facility and must consider what impact
the incinerator may have on the environment.

But where land is scarce, resource recovery facilities
may be the most economical choice. When the re-

source recovery plant in Saugus, Massachusetts, opened in 1976 it was charging $13 a ton, which was much higher than the $9 a ton charged by the landfills. Now, even though the tipping fees at the plant have risen to $22 a ton, they are a bargain compared to the $60 per ton tipping fee at landfills.

Clearly, the resource recovery industry in the United States is going to be a vital part of any solid-waste management program of the future. However, to be the best it can be, research is still needed concerning the effectiveness of pollution-control equipment and the impact of chemicals on the environment and on human health. Also, the government must maintain vigilance over existing plants. There are still many incinerators in the United States that are known to be operating poorly, yet they have not been shut down. It seems to be easier for the EPA to be tough on industry than to deal with municipalities.

5

RECYCLING—MINING URBAN WASTES

The United States hasn't always been a throwaway society. When the country was young and materials of any kind were scarce or expensive, a "waste not, want not" ethic prevailed. Women saved the wax drippings from their candles. Boys got jobs cleaning off old bricks with hatchets or pounding used nails to straighten them out.

The national interest in recycling was also strong during our participation in the two world wars. Americans pulled together to salvage anything that would contribute to the war effort. Waste material went into the building of guns, planes, tanks, and ships. Patriotic citizens collected scrap iron, other scrap metals, wastepaper, scrap rubber, and cotton and woolen rags. In the fall and summer of 1942, an average of 450,000 cars a month were taken out of auto graveyards so that their scrap metal could be turned into war materials.

Rubber was in short supply during World War II after the Japanese overran Southeast Asia and captured almost 90 percent of the natural rubber production. Americans began turning in scrap rubber, from old tires to bathing caps, heels, and even rubber bands.

Recycling the metal from old automobiles
is not only economical, it prevents the eyesore
of unattractive automobile graveyards.

When the war ended, so did America's interest in recycling. The country became more affluent. Its citizens were more interested in convenience than in saving. With everything in abundance, most people saw no reason to recycle. For the most part, it was cheaper to make things from raw materials than from recycled products.

Another surge of interest in recycling came in the early 1970s. Max Spendlove, a research director with the U.S. Bureau of Mines, popularized the term "urban ore." He claimed that our waste was a rich source of iron, aluminum, copper, zinc, tin, lead, and brass that should be "mined."

At first the idea of "mining urban ore," or recycling, received an enthusiastic response. Engineers created new machinery to collect reusable materials and to burn what was left for energy. But the results of the recycling effort did not prove as successful as its promoters had hoped. Big resource recovery plants suffered delays, breakdowns, and continuing financial loss. Markets for the recycled materials were poor. After a while, nobody talked much about mining the urban ore.

THE GROWING NEED
FOR RECYCLING

There has been renewed interest in recycling in the past several years, mainly because of the critical shortage of landfill space. People also see recycling as a way to save resources and energy.

With landfills closing at the rate of nearly one a day and the cost of incineration going up, it becomes clear that every item saved from the dumpsite is significant. The life of existing landfills can be stretched by first removing from our trash those materials that have market value. By reducing the amount of trash to be dealt with, recycling programs ultimately provide tax savings for local residents.

Most of our methods of disposing of waste don't attempt to recover any of the valuable materials it contains. Yet, in our trash cans, landfills, and incinerators there are valuable natural resources. According to David Morris of the Institute for Local Self Reliance, "A city the size of San Francisco disposes of more aluminum than is produced by a small bauxite mine, more copper than a medium copper mine, and more paper than a good-sized timber stand."

Minerals take thousands and even millions of years to form. Once they are used up, they are gone. Even renewable resources, such as wood pulp, may take 50 to 150 years to renew. Since many of our raw materials must be imported from other countries, the United States is at the mercy of countries who may cut off our supply or raise prices to extreme levels. Recycling can help make us less dependent on these foreign producers and at the same time help us preserve our own natural resources.

Experts believe that half of the nearly 160 million tons of municipal garbage thrown away each year could easily be recycled, and that as much as 80 percent could be with greater efforts. The EPA has set a more modest goal of recycling 25 percent of our waste by 1992. Presently, only about 10 percent of the nation's garbage is being recycled, compared to as much as 60 percent by some cities in Europe and Japan.

PROBLEMS WITH RECYCLING

Although the concept of recycling in order to save natural resources and reduce the waste stream is good, the process is not without problems. Before waste products can be recycled, they need to be separated into similar materials. This is expensive if done by hand at some central point and inconvenient if done by householders.

The inconvenience involved in recycling is one reason more people don't participate in recycling programs. Americans are used to throwing things away and generally are not interested in spending the time and effort needed for recycling. They don't want to go to the trouble of separating their garbage into recyclable and non-recyclable parts or rinsing out their bottles and cans. They are in the habit of throwing all their trash into one can, and old habits are hard to break. Some states, such as Connecticut, Oregon, New Jersey, and Pennsylvania, have found that the only way to change these attitudes is to make recycling mandatory.

The other main problem with recycling is that the demand for recycled products has yet to match the supply. Unless there is a market to absorb the materials, the added efforts have been wasted. In some communities, recycling programs that were expected to generate revenue backfired. The communities ended up with piles of materials with no one to sell them to. The materials still ended up in the landfill, and the communities had to pay for both recycling *and* dumping.

Markets for recycled products are inconsistent. The demand for certain materials changes from month to month, causing fluctuations in their price. The amounts paid for such items as scrap iron, copper, and old newsprint are notoriously changeable. Aggressive recycling programs can produce a glut of certain materials. The market for used newspapers in the Northeast has already become so flooded that some communities have to pay brokers to haul them away. In the past, the brokers were paying the communities for their paper.

69

Another thing that has hurt markets is the reluctance of some industry officials to used recycled raw materials. They are concerned about the uniform quality of those materials. But there are many instances where using recycled products would only slightly change the quality of a product. For instance, egg cartons and meat packaging trays used to be made of pulp, which required a very low grade of paper. This made them an ideal candidate for using recycled paper. But today, most of these packages have been replaced by plastic foam containers that are not easily broken down. These foam products not only clog our landfills, they also eliminate a good market for recycled paper.

Markets for recycled materials are expected to stabilize as the recycling industry grows. In the meantime, some states are doing their part by requiring government agencies to buy products made from recycled materials when they are available. Some states are also giving tax incentives to businesses that use recyclable materials in their manufacturing processes. Oregon pioneered the use of tax incentives over twenty years ago. The program has paid off. The state now recovers 25 percent of its trash and has one of the most successful recycling industries in the country.

Communities need to look at recycling in a different light to see its real benefit. Citizens have been hampered by the belief that recycling programs should make money. In reality, aluminum is the only material that is consistently profitable. The real financial benefit to most communities is not the amount of money earned from selling recycled materials but the money saved by keeping those materials out of the crowded landfills.

Running a weekly curbside trash collection and recycling program costs on the average of $20 to $30 a ton. It is doubtful that a community can get that much back by selling the materials collected. However, it would cost them some $40 to $60 a ton to haul trash to a landfill, and $70 to $120 a ton to burn it. The amount the community saves in disposal costs needs to be considered part of the profit from its recycling program. Whether or not recycling makes economic sense to a community depends on how much it is paying to dispose of its waste, what markets are available for the recovered products, and the expense involved in operating the recycling program.

IMPLEMENTING
RECYCLING PROGRAMS

In order for any recycling program to be successful it must first gain the cooperation of the residents to assure a sufficient supply of recyclable materials. But it is not easy to get people to change their habits, especially where trash is concerned. Many Americans have the attitude that waste is useless stuff and are only concerned with getting rid of it as cheaply as possible. Therefore, the first step in a recycling program is public education. Residents need to know what benefits recycling will bring to their community. They also need to have a clear understanding of what to do, how to do it, when to do it, and where to do it. To spread awareness, the EPA has provided a $200,000 grant to the U.S. Environmental Fund/Ad Council campaign to promote recycling nationwide.

The second requirement for a successful recycling program is convenience. Perhaps the greatest inconvenience for recyclers is separating the materials. At one extreme, contractors can sort through the trash after it has all been picked up. However, this is an expensive procedure because of the labor involved. A more efficient way is for residents and businesses to separate the materials at their source before everything is crushed together in sanitation trucks.

To make source separation convenient, some communities give their citizens colorful, space-saving storage containers. One color is for newspapers, another for aluminum, and a third for glass. These containers are set out next to the rest of the trash. Trash collectors put the recyclable materials into special bins on their trucks and the rest of the trash into the compactor compartment. The colored containers are highly visible to neighbors, so more residents feel obligated to take part in the program. A system such as this has helped Marin County, north of San Francisco, California, keep some 300 truckloads of waste out of their landfills every month. This 6 percent reduction in the volume of waste extends the life of their landfill and gives the county government more time to find other solutions.

Getting people into the habit of recycling often takes incentives. Most incentives involve money—either bonuses for participating or fines for not participating. Container deposit laws are used in many states to encourage consumers to bring back the bottles and cans their beverages come in. In Seattle, the incentive to recycle is provided by the promise of lower collection costs. Residents are charged according to the number of refuse containers they set out for collection. The more they have, the more they pay for. Recycling cuts down on the amount to be thrown away, so it saves the residents money.

WE'RE GETTING BETTER

More state and local governments are setting up recycling programs to ease the volume of waste flowing into their crowded landfills. In 1989 more than 500 cities had regular curbside collection of recyclable materials,

Color-coded storage containers make
recycling more convenient. It's simple
enough for even the youngest citizens.

twice that of five years earlier. At the same time, ten states had made recycling mandatory. New Jersey is one such state. Its residents produce 13.5 million tons of solid waste each year, with 92 percent of it going to sixteen landfills. By 1985, all of these landfills contained 25 percent more than they were intended to. Recycling was made mandatory to alleviate the problem.

Improved technology has also made recycling more convenient. In 1989 a plant opened in Rhode Island that can sort mixed household trash for recycling. As the trash is carried along on a conveyor belt, an electromagnet picks up tin-plated steel cans and carries them off to be shredded. The remaining trash passes through a rolling curtain of chains, which light aluminum and plastic can't pass through. The aluminum is separated out using electric current that creates a magnetic field in the aluminum objects. The plastic objects are further sorted into hard containers, such as milk jugs, and softer ones, such as soft drink bottles. The only thing that is separated by hand is glass, which must be put into groups according to color—green, amber, and clear. This plant is designed to process more than 80 tons a day of mixed recyclables using six workers.

Another invention to make recycling easier is the reverse vending machine. Recyclable materials, such as aluminum cans, can be fed into the machine by consumers. The machine issues either cash or a redeemable voucher. Most reverse vending machines are for aluminum cans and plastic bottles, but some accepting glass are on the market.

Even in its first year, Seattle's recycling program far exceeded its goals when 60 percent of the households in the city of about 500,000 participated. Nearly 30 percent of the garbage is recycled. Residents of Seattle have door-to-door pickup for materials to be recycled. Their papers, bottles, and cans are taken to two recycling plants, where they are sorted. The newspapers are shipped to Asia and processed into newsprint. The rest of the paper, including everything from junk mail to egg cartons, is shipped to South Korea, where it is made into cheap insulation and filler for cardboard. Glass bottles and cans made from aluminum and tin are sent to brokers handling those materials. As an experiment, plastics are being sent to Thailand, where they are cleaned and reprocessed into everything from toothbrush handles to car parts. Seattle's next step will be to offer low-cost pickup of yard wastes such as grass clippings, leaves, branches, and so on. These will be processed into compost and sold to nurseries.

Seattle has also enlisted cooperation from its businesses, which generally throw out two-thirds of the recycled materials and generate more than half of the city's trash. Seattle's two commercial trash haulers will give customers a reduced rate if they separate their recyclable materials. As an added step to help its crowded landfills, city facilities in Seattle no longer use Styrofoam products because they are nonbiodegradable.

Some cities have come up with ingenious solutions to special problems. New Orleans has found a way to recycle thousands of Christmas trees, which normally end up in landfills, dumps, or on vacant property. In 1988 Louisiana state officials began sinking 1,000 evergreens into the marshes along Lake Pontchartrain to form an underwater dike to slow the erosion that has been eating away 50 square miles of Louisiana coastline annually. The next Christmas, 7,000 trees were added to the marsh. The city plans to make this a yearly event.

Fort Worth, Texas, keeps its Christmas trees out of landfills by chipping them into mulch for use at city facilities. The city has a special pickup for the trees. The program was expected to bring in 16,000 trees its first year. Instead, collectors ended up getting 24,000, enough to add two weeks to the life of their landfill.

75

WHAT NEEDS TO BE DONE

There are not nearly enough programs designed to reduce waste volumes and to encourage recycling. Businesses, governments, and consumers will have to work together to bring about the needed changes.

There will not be any significant reduction in our incredible volume of waste until manufacturers begin designing products and packages for durability, reuse, and recycling. Right now, most product designers are facing the pressure of cost control, international competition, and the need to make their products distinct. Most are not concerned with making their products recyclable. Someday, state and local governments may try to force companies to use more recycled materials in their products or to make their own products recyclable. But for now, most companies don't want to go to the extra expense of making these changes.

In one instance, consumer opposition to nonrecyclable packaging paid off. The National Coalition for Recyclable Waste, a Washington-based consumer group, fought against the new plastic Coca-Cola can. Recyclers were concerned that the polyvinyl chloride label would contribute to dioxin formation if the cans were burned. And since the plastic cans looked very much like their aluminum counterparts, they could mistakenly be mixed in with the aluminum cans at recycling plants. The cans could cause sudden flares that could damage the smelters. Largely because of public pressure, Coca-Cola has sidelined its plans for the plastic cans until more research can be done.

Local governments can help the recycling effort by requiring that any contracts given to waste collectors and haulers include a comprehensive curbside recycling program. Some cities already do this, but it is far from being a general practice. The cities most likely to use this tactic are ones that face skyrocketing waste-disposal costs. Sometimes, environmentally conscious residents demand it.

Municipalities with extremely high waste-disposal costs can adopt a system of "shared savings" that would make money for both the city and the recyclers. For example, in Philadelphia a ton of recyclable newsprint sells for $20 to $25. But the cost of disposing of that newsprint is $90 a ton. If the city paid recyclers half its avoided costs—$45—both sides would come out ahead.

Governments on all levels can help open up markets for recyclable materials. One portion of the Resource Conservation and Recovery Act (RCRA) of 1976 requires all levels of government and government contractors to purchase items containing the highest percentage of recovered materials practicable. However, the drawing up of guidelines has been slow. Governments consume incredible amounts of materials and products of all types. They could contribute heavily to the market of recycled materials if they used recycled paper for their reports, laws, and tax forms; if they heated government complexes with waste oil; and if they paved roads with material using recovered rubber.

RECYCLING SPECIFIC MATERIALS

Aluminum. The process of producing aluminum from bauxite ore takes a great deal of energy, more than for any other material that we commonly use. But 95 percent of that energy can be saved by recycling aluminum. Each ton of remelted aluminum saves four tons of bauxite and 1,500 pounds (700 kg) of petroleum coke and pitch, which are used in the process. Each ton reduces the amount of air-polluting aluminum fluoride by 77 pounds (35 kg).

Aluminum is one of the most popular, and profitable, materials recycled by Americans. A survey done by the Institute of Scrap Recycling Industries found that in 1988, 54.6 percent of the aluminum cans were recycled compared to 50.5 percent from 1987. That amounts to 42.5 billion aluminum cans recycled in 1988 compared to 36.5 billion cans in 1987. Other studies indicate that the average can that comes out of the store will be re-melted and back on the shelves within six weeks. Over a billion dollars have been paid to Americans for their efforts.

Paper. The biggest market for recyclables is paper. It makes up approximately 41 percent of the waste stream and has been recycled for generations. The American Paper Institute estimated that, in 1988, the United States would recover 26.5 million tons of waste paper, including everything from high-quality computer paper to newspapers, corrugated cardboard, and junk mail.

The environmental impact of recycling paper is great. The process not only saves valuable forests, it requires up to three-quarters less energy and uses only half as much water as making the paper from virgin timber. In 1984, paper-recycling programs in nine industrial countries spared a million acres of trees. Just recycling the two million copies of a Sunday edition of the *New York Times* would save 75,000 trees.

Glass. Refillable glass bottles are the most energy-efficient beverage containers on the market because they only require a thorough washing before reuse. These bottles are about 50 percent heavier than the non-refillable bottles and can be used up to thirty times. Refillable glass bottles are used more in European countries than they are in the United States. In the Netherlands, 95 percent of retail soft drinks and 90 percent of beer is sold in returnable bottles.

Above and over: recycling newspapers and aluminum cans saves energy and natural resources while also keeping that same trash out of the landfills.

Crushed glass, called *cullet,* can be used to make new glass. For every ton of cullet used in the manufacturing process, about 1.2 tons of raw materials are saved. The use of cullet also reduces the energy needed for manufacturing and the amount of air pollution caused by it.

Plastic. By weight, more plastics are produced in the United States than aluminum and all other nonferrous metals combined. Foam coffee cups and fast food containers; disposable diapers, pens, and razors; plastic wrap; toys; and countless other plastic items account for about 7 percent of the total weight of our waste stream, or about 10.5 million tons annually. The percentage is expected to rise to 10 percent by the year 2000. Yet out of this tremendous amount, only 1 percent of all plastic waste is being recycled.

The large quantity of plastic in the waste stream presents special problems. Some types, mainly PVC, can give off toxic chemicals such as dioxin when they are burned in incinerators. When dumped in landfills, they can remain there virtually forever because they are not biodegradable. Although some effort is now being made to mix cornstarch with plastic to make it biodegradable, currently this amounts to no more than 0.5 percent of all plastic products in the United States.

Recycling plastic is more difficult than recycling most other materials. Part of the problem is that plastic is not a single material. There are more than 46 different types of plastic in common use, and visually distinguishing one plastic resin from another is difficult. Also, some products are made up of several layers, with each layer consisting of a different type of plastic. Therefore, it is difficult to separate plastics according to type, and few recycling processes can handle more than one type.

Some states now require plastic products to be imprinted with an identification number indicating what type of resin was used. This will make it easier to separate the plastics into similar types so they may be recycled.

Because plastics are clogging our landfills, many states are considering some kind of ban or restriction on nonrecyclable plastics such as those used in fast-food containers and disposable diapers. Minneapolis and St. Paul have already passed laws to prohibit nonbiodegradable and nonrecyclable plastic food containers beginning in 1990.

In spite of its difficulties, the plastics recycling business is beginning to grow in the United States. Some companies are finding uses for soft drink bottles made from polyethylene terephthalate (PET). U.S. consumers throw away 750 million pounds (340 million kg) of these plastic soda bottles a year, but at this time, only 20 percent, or 150 million pounds (68 million kg), are being recycled. Almost all of these recycled bottles come from the nine states with bottle-deposit laws.

Although it is still not possible to turn a used PET bottle into a new one, other uses have been found for them. Some plastic bottles are shredded and stuffed into seat cushions or used as insulation in sleeping bags and jackets. In East Germany, PET bottles are turned into polyester backing for carpets and other textiles.

Another type of plastic that is clogging our landfills is polystyrene foam, the type that is found in meat trays and fast food containers. Some areas have already banned the use of these products. In order to avoid having their products banned, some plastics manufacturers are experimenting with recycling foam containers by shredding them into pea-size pellets for use in wall insulation and industrial packaging. A Massachusetts company will clean up and break down the foam products and turn them into a plastic resin that can be formed into new items such as flowerpots, wall insulation, and coat hangers.

In one recycling process, mixed plastics, including polystyrene foam, can be turned into durable fence posts and pier supports. The factory shreds plastics into flakes, then washes and separates them from remnants of bottle caps and paper labels. Then the material is pressed into plastic lumber. These plastic logs don't rust or rot and are said to have an almost unlimited life span. Their use is being encouraged in Japan, where the use of plastic is soaring and wood supplies are limited.

TIRES

There are an estimated 2 billion used tires cluttering up the United States and over 200 million—equal to some 12 million tons—are added to the pile each year. Most public landfills don't accept tires or they charge high fees to take them because they take up so much room. Most of them end up in huge unsightly mounds in tire dumps. These tires are not only ugly, they also serve as breeding grounds for rodents and mosquitoes, and are a fire hazard. A few are recycled in old-fashioned ways, such as retreading them or turning them into backyard tire swings or buffers for marine and truck loading docks. Now, more of an effort is being made to find other uses for them.

The problem with recycling tires is that it is difficult to separate the rubber from the steel belts. The process costs so much that it is not economical for some uses. A California company plans to incinerate 45,000 tons of tires (4.5 million) annually, to generate 14.4 megawatts of electrical power. This company has access to the nation's largest stockpile of tires in Modesto, California, which at last count had about 35 million tires weighing some 350,000 tons.

Another company thinks that there should be a better way to use the mounds of rubber than just burning them for energy. They have come up with a process where they can turn old rubber into a finely ground powder, which can be blended with polyethylene plastic, then molded into products ranging from milk crates to automotive bumper guards. The initial use of this mixture may be in safety cones and barriers for roads and highways because many states now require their agencies to buy recycled materials when they are priced competitively.

In New Jersey, tires are being ground into crumb rubber and mixed with asphalt to be used on roads. Besides getting rid of unwanted tires, this process creates a road surface that is more durable than regular paving material. The road surface is also said to be more skid and abrasion resistant.

COMPOSTING

Next to paper, the second-largest component in our waste stream is yard waste—grass clippings, tree trimmings, fallen leaves, and so on. The 28.6 million tons of yard wastes produced every year amount to 18 percent of the waste stream. This tremendous volume puts a strain on our already overcrowded landfills.

For years farmers have been in the habit of putting leaves, garbage, animal manures, and other organic wastes into dirt piles to produce compost, a soil conditioner. Now, some communities have begun using this method as a means of keeping yard wastes out of their landfills.

In composting, organic matter such as yard wastes, garbage, sewage sludge, and so on, is mixed into piles of dirt and allowed to decompose. During this process, the volume of the waste is reduced to about one-third its original weight. The end product is a humuslike material, useful as a soil conditioner. It can be used by communities to cover landfills; as mulch for roadsides and parks; or sold to nurseries and landscapers. Some compost is even turned into a base material for more refined products such as fertilizers, wallboards, or building blocks. However, unless governments make deliberate efforts to put composted material to use, markets are hard to find.

Although, theoretically, composting is a good way of recovering resources from solid waste, it is not suitable for use in large metropolitan areas where the cost of the land makes it too expensive. Instead of setting up city-wide composting projects, some areas, such as the state of New Jersey, have outlawed yard wastes in landfills, requiring homeowners to cope as best they can. Some communities, such as Brookhaven, New York, turn their yard waste into compost at a community center. Householders are given the compost free of charge. This system more than pays for itself by the $4 million or so that is avoided in landfill costs.

Some landfills could presumably save money on the cost of landfill cover if they practiced composting. For example, the Fresh Kills Landfill on Staten Island in New York must pay more than $7 per cubic meter to have cover material shipped to the landfill. Once this material is delivered, it takes up about 17 percent of the landfill area. If compost were made at Fresh Kills it could remove almost 2,000 tons of garbage from the waste stream and eliminate the cost of transporting cover material.

In spite of new programs for its use, composting in the United States may never be as widespread as it is in Europe. France alone has over a hundred plants producing 800,000 tons of compost each year. Much of it is used in the vineyards. Composting can be especially valuable in arid regions with sandy soils because compost helps to retain moisture in the soil. Countries on the dry Arabian Peninsula compost much of their own solid waste but still import more from European countries.

Recycling, whether it is household trash or yard wastes, will undoubtably become a fact of life in the future for most of the country. At the present time, at least, it appears to be the only way to significantly reduce our waste stream and to extend the lives of our overcrowded landfills.

6

OCEAN DUMPING

During the summer of 1988, when thousands of New Yorkers went to the beach to get relief from the sweltering heat, they did not find a refreshing ocean. Instead, they found a disgusting array of wastes floating in the water and littering the beaches. Among other things, the trash included balls of sewage 2 inches (5 cm) thick, dead laboratory rats, and even a human stomach lining. Drug paraphernalia and medical wastes such as needles and syringes, stained bandages, and containers of surgical sutures washed ashore. Even more alarming were dozen of vials of blood, three of which tested positive for hepatitis-B virus and at least six of which tested positive for antibodies to the AIDS virus. Various beaches were closed to swimmers off and on all summer.

HISTORY OF OCEAN DUMPING

For hundreds, even thousands, of years, societies around the world have dumped garbage into oceans. Both commercial and military ships threw garbage and other wastes overboard. Municipalities that had little space to use for landfills used the ocean as a dump. Those who did the dumping had a clear conscience, because it was assumed that the vast ocean could handle anything put into it.

Times have changed, and so has the nature of solid waste. Today, there are more chemicals and toxic materials in our trash that can harm the natural state of the ocean. There are more floating wastes, especially plastics, which can wash ashore and foul the beaches.

The rampant population growth along the coasts of the United States has contributed to the problem. In 1940 the number of Americans living within 50 miles (80 km) of a seashore was estimated at 42 million. By 1980 that figure had more than doubled to 89 million, and the number keeps increasing. It is no wonder that our oceans are taking a beating. Coastal waters are rapidly reaching their capacity to absorb civilization's wastes.

The once popular practice of dumping raw garbage and trash into the ocean began to decline in the United States in the 1950s due to public pressure and local ordinances. Today, no municipal waste is dumped into the ocean.

To help protect the oceans, two acts were passed in the 1970s. The U.S. Ocean Dumping Act of 1972 and the International Dumping at Sea Act of 1974 both banned ocean dumping of many of the components of garbage and trash, including metals from printers' inks, plastics, wood, radioactive wastes, and biological and chemical warfare agents. Now, if the United States ever wants to implement ocean dumping it will first have to get international approval.

Just because the practice of dumping municipal solid waste into the ocean has stopped doesn't mean that the oceans are free of refuse. For about fifty years, New York City dumped its sewage sludge at several sites 12 miles (19 km) off the entrance to New York Harbor. But

Beaches look more like dumps when strewn with trash from passing boats and litter left by careless beachgoers.

in 1985, the EPA issued a directive stating that the dumping of sewage sludge had to be moved to a site 106 miles (170 km) offshore. New York and New Jersey then began barging their sludge 106 miles out and releasing it underwater. Even this became unacceptable. A more recent federal law will totally ban sludge dumping at sea by 1992. Some of the alternatives being studied include transforming sludge into artificial soil, injecting it deep into the earth, and incinerating it.

In addition to sludge, the oceans are the trash dumps for thousands of ships crisscrossing the waters. Nearly all the trash from the world's commercial fleet is thrown into the ocean with little or no prior treatment. This is no small amount. According to the Department of Labor, in 1986 there were 25,580 ships in the world fleet with combined crews totaling more than 625,000. In 1975 the National Academy of Sciences estimated that about 7 million tons of trash were discarded into the ocean each year from passenger ships, merchant and military ships, commercial fishing boats, and recreational craft. This figure didn't include garbage. Most of the waste was paper, followed by metal, cloth, glass, and small percentages of plastics and rubber.

IMPORTANCE OF OCEANS

To some people, ocean dumping may seem like a good idea. It is inexpensive—no need for expensive landfills and incinerators—just some barges and tugboats will do. There is little chance that the air or groundwater will become polluted. Also, there is no serious threat from the NIMBY syndrome. But on taking a closer look, it becomes clear that the world's oceans are too important to take chances with.

The ocean covers over 70 percent of the earth's surface and is the principal source of food for 10 percent of the world's population. Unfortunately, it is also the final destination for almost all pollutants disposed of. Much of the contamination comes from the chemicals that find their way into the ocean from coastal industries and from inadequate sewage treatment. Other dangerous chemicals come from agricultural runoffs, where fertilizers and pesticides wash into streams and rivers and eventually reach the ocean. Even pollutants in the air can eventually end up there through precipitation. For decades these chemical and metal discharges have poured largely unchecked into the world's oceans. They have poisoned millions of fish and left millions of others unfit to eat.

Marine biologists and environmentalists feel that ocean pollution is reaching epidemic proportions. The wastes and chemicals being dumped directly or indirectly into the sea are threatening marine life. The pollution is making a day at some beaches about as pleasant as swimming in an unflushed toilet. It is also creating financial losses for those who make their living from the fishing and tourist industries. Perhaps even more important than the billions of dollars that are being lost is the damage pollution does to the quality of life.

It was once assumed that throwing trash into the ocean was harmless because nutrients in the waste would increase production of fish and shellfish. Now we know that even garbage, which is organic, can have a detrimental effect on marine life. Rotting garbage consumes oxygen dissolved in the water. If too much oxygen is used up in a particular area, there is not enough left to keep fish alive. Another problem is that garbage-eating fish may ingest bacteria and viruses that are associated with wastes. If these same fish are eaten raw, they can cause illness in humans.

The oceans are also affected by the dumping of solid wastes from ships. One hazard of dumping raw, unprocessed, unsorted garbage and trash into the ocean is that today our trash contains a high percentage of float-ables that create a mess that is not only ugly to us but threatening to marine life. Each year as many as two million seabirds and 100,000 marine mammals die after eating or becoming entangled in debris. Sea turtles can choke on plastic bags that they mistake for jellyfish. Sea lions may playfully poke their noses through plastic nets and rings and may starve to death because they can't open their mouths.

Of course, not all the plastic debris on the beaches washes in from the oceans. Most of it is left behind by careless beachgoers. Texas got tired of its cluttered beaches and started its "Adopt-A-Beach" program. Groups volunteer to "adopt" a section of beach and see that it is kept clean. During the Great Texas Beach Trash Off of 1989, nearly 4,700 volunteers scoured 136 miles (219 km) of Texas beaches and collected 121 tons of trash.

INCINERATION AT SEA

The ocean has been seen by some as the ideal place to incinerate hazardous wastes that must be burned at extremely high temperatures. Conducting this process at sea has two advantages. For one thing, it eliminates opposition from residents who are adamantly opposed to having hazardous wastes burned anywhere near their neighborhoods. Furthermore, burning hazardous waste at sea is much cheaper. Some wastes give off extreme amounts of hydrogen chloride when they burn. In land-based incinerators, expensive scrubbers must be used in the chimneys to collect the gas and neutralize it. But the ocean is naturally alkaline and can absorb and neutralize the hydrogen chloride by itself.

In spite of these advantages, there is only one place in the world where chemical waste is regularly incin-

The plastic rings around beverage containers can cause death in fish and marine life that get caught in them.

Volunteers cleaned up 136 miles
(219 km) of Texas beaches during the
Great Texas Beach Trashoff.

erated at sea. About 100 miles (160 km) off the north-eastern coast of England the incinerator ship, *Vulcanus II*, burns some 110,000 to 120,000 tons of waste a year. Most of it comes from West Germany. However, be-cause of pressure by environmentalists, burning waste at sea will probably be stopped by 1994 because of an agreement signed by European governments.

At one time, hazardous waste from the United States was incinerated at sea. In 1982, *Vulcanus* was given permission by the EPA to burn 3.6 million gallons (13.6 million l) of PCBs in the Gulf of Mexico, off the Texas coast. It reportedly destroyed over 99 percent of the PCBs it burned that year, but angry protesters were worried that the leftover one percent might blow in-land. Public pressure eventually convinced authorities to ban incineration at sea near the United States.

PROTECTING OUR OCEANS

Nations are working together to try to stop the harmful effects of waste disposal in oceans. Many nations, in-cluding the United States, have ratified an amendment to the MARPOL (Marine Pollution) treaty. This amend-ment prohibits ships and boats from disposing of plas-tics anywhere in the oceans. The pact went into effect at the end of 1988. As with many pollution controls, this new policy will be expensive and difficult to imple-ment for some. It means that the merchant ships will not be able to dump their usual 450,000 plastic con-tainers overboard every day. It means that the U.S. Navy will have to find another means of disposing of the 4 tons of plastic waste it gets rid of daily. The navy began its compliance by canceling a contract for 11 million plastic shopping bags. It is also testing a shipboard trash compactor and a waste processor that can melt plastic and turn it into bricks. It is expected to cost the navy at least $1 million per ship to meet the provisions of the treaty.

THE FUTURE OF OCEAN DUMPING

With the solid-waste disposal problem reaching crisis proportions in some areas, some studies have been done to see if ocean dumping could be resumed. So far, no municipality has recommended this as a viable solution because no one can say with certainty just how it would affect the ocean's ecology. However, there are some types of waste that might be acceptable. For instance, researchers are using blocks of stabilized incinerator ash to build artificial fishing reefs to attract marine life.

In the future, a closer look may have to be taken at ocean dumping. No matter how efficient the country becomes at recycling and resource recovery, there will always be waste left over that has to be put somewhere. Since it is unlikely that anyone will figure out a way to dispose of waste in the air, the land and the sea are the only two places left. It is possible that the improved technology that has helped create our waste problems may also be used to find safe ways to dispose of some forms of waste in the ocean. Ocean dumping should only be resumed, if at all, when enough research has been done to determine its total effect on the ecology of our oceans. It should never be done merely to appease the "out of sight, out of mind" attitude toward trash.

7

WHEN WASTE IS DANGEROUS

The residents of the quiet Niagara Falls, New York, neighborhood were proud of where they lived. Trees lined the streets, children played outside in neatly groomed yards, and everyone seemed happy. Then strange things began to happen. People started getting sick, complaining of nervous disorders and liver problems. Trees turned black. The air was filled with a foul odor and oozing slime burned holes in children's shoes. More pregnant women than normal were having miscarriages, and many of the babies that were born had birth defects. Upon investigation the alarmed residents learned that they were living next to a toxic waste dump with the gentle-sounding name, Love Canal.

The problem actually began in the 1930s when a chemical company dumped steel drums filled with waste chemicals into the Love Canal. In the 1950s the company covered the canal with clay and earth and donated the land to Niagara Falls. Homes and schools were built up around the edge of the canal. A few years later, homeowners found a strange black liquid seeping into their basements. An investigation showed that the dangerous chemicals had leaked out of the drums and had found their way through the ground to nearby homes.

Among the two hundred compounds found in the waste, twelve were known to be carcinogenic, or cancer causing. The area had become such an unhealthy place to live that finally, in 1980, President Carter signed a bill to permanently move more than eight hundred families out of Love Canal.

The tragedy of Love Canal alerted the United States to the danger of chemical dumps, even those that have long been closed and forgotten. Now the nearly impossible task has begun of cleaning up waste sites and preventing more dangerous chemical dumps from being built.

HAZARDOUS WASTE

The United States generates an awesome 300 million tons of hazardous waste every year. Several things can make waste hazardous. Some types can ignite, starting fires and creating heat and smoke that could release harmful particles into the environment. Others can corrode and be released into the environment by eating through their containers. Some chemicals are hazardous because they react with air, water, or other chemicals to the point that they are explosive. Toxic wastes can poison humans or give them cancer. Infectious wastes from hospitals and medical laboratories can infect people, animals, or plants with diseases. Highly active nuclear waste gives off radiation that can harm even future generations. It is too dangerous even to dispose of.

TOXIC WASTE

Toxic waste makes up the largest portion of our hazardous waste stream. Most toxic waste comes from industry, especially the chemical industry. Much of it is

Wastewater discharge from a chemical company's processing facility and incinerator flows into a nearby river.

dumped in landfills or in pits, ponds, or lagoons. Until 1976, when Congress passed strict laws regulating the dumping of toxic wastes, many of them were stored in metal drums that were dumped in landfills or garbage dumps along with municipal solid waste. As a result, many of the older landfills are a stew of haphazardly mixed chemicals. Since records were not required, no one even knows what chemicals these landfills may contain.

Not all the toxic waste being thrown out improperly comes from industry. Even common household trash contains some hazardous chemicals. Discarded cleaning fluids, pesticides, paint thinners, batteries, and battery acids are just a few of the chemicals tossed into trash cans that eventually find their way into landfills. For example, twenty-eight million car batteries are put into landfills or incinerators each year. From these come 260,000 tons of hazardous lead. Some states are trying to limit the number of discarded batteries. Rhode Island has started charging a deposit on car batteries to encourage their return when they die. New York bans automobile and household batteries from its incinerators.

Perhaps what the toxic chemical environmentalists fear most is dioxin, a by-product of the manufacture of certain weed killers and several other industrial processes. Dioxin can cause health problems such as headaches, stomachaches, and a severe skin rash called chloracne. Some researchers also believe that dioxin may cause birth defects and cancer. Dioxin is difficult to get rid of because it does not readily break down in soil or water. The only effective way to destroy it is to burn it at very high temperatures.

Dioxin disrupted the lives of the 2,200 residents of the small town of Times Beach, Missouri. In the early 1970s, used oil was sprayed on dirt roads in the area to keep down the dust. At the time no one knew that the oil was severely contaminated with dioxin. Twelve years later, in 1982, floods washed the dioxin into town and threatened the health of everyone who lived there. Although the government paid to relocate the residents of Times Beach, many of these people still worry that someday they might develop cancer from their exposure to dioxin.

MANAGING TOXIC WASTE

Now that the cheap and easy landfilling of toxic waste is illegal, the federal government has adopted a "waste-management hierarchy" as a guide to improving industrial hazardous waste-management practices.

Source reduction. The first stage in getting rid of toxic waste is to reduce the amount that is being produced. Companies can be encouraged to change their manufacturing processes so that they use fewer chemicals and reuse chemicals whenever possible. This can be expensive but in the long run may be cheaper than paying for the safe disposal of their toxic waste. One company that has done this successfully is 3M Minnesota Mining and Manufacturing Co., makers of Scotch Tape and other products. The company has cut in half the amount of hazardous waste it generates by separating out the substances that can be reused and by substituting safer raw materials for hazardous ones. In 1988, its changes saved the company $420 million.

Recycling. Recycling toxic waste reduces the amount that must be disposed of. This method was not used much in the past, when it was cheaper to dispose of the waste and use new raw materials. But today the cost of energy, raw materials, and waste disposal are all rising rapidly. Industries are finally realizing the economic benefits of recycling their hazardous waste.

Townspeople gather to promote a reduction in the generation of toxic waste. Less toxic waste to begin with means less of it that has to be disposed of properly.

In many cases the "waste" from one industry may serve as the raw materials for another. A California company found that "pickling acid," which is used in metal-processing plants to remove scale, could be mixed with zinc sulfate and used as a soil additive in citrus orchards.

In order to help companies find someone who wants their waste products, three nonprofit organizations have been set up in the United States to do some "matchmaking." These organizations compile lists of companies looking for certain materials and lists of companies trying to get rid of materials. By comparing lists, buyers and sellers can find each other.

Treatment. Many wastes can be treated to reduce or eliminate their toxicity. Acids and caustics can be neutralized and, if not otherwise contaminated, safely drained into sewers. This often allows two wastes to be taken care of at one time.

Incineration. Some toxins, such as organic solvents, PCBs, and dioxin, can only be broken down when burned at temperatures exceeding 2,400° F (1,316° C). When this is done, the incinerators must be closely regulated to be sure that their temperatures don't fall below this level, resulting in toxic gases being released into the air. Emissions from smokestacks must also be regulated.

Some companies have developed portable incinerators that can be taken to contaminated areas such as Love Canal or Times Beach. One company uses a mobile electric reactor that can heat up to 4,000° F (2,204° C)—hot enough to destroy the dioxin in several hundred pounds of soil. The EPA also has a mobile incinerator that was used at Times Beach. Within six weeks, it got rid of 99.9 percent of the dioxin in 1,750 gallons (6,624 liters) of liquid waste and 40 tons of soil.

103

Cement companies have found that by burning hazardous waste in their kilns they can save money on fuel and also get paid for eliminating some dangerous chemicals. The huge kilns are used to turn limestone into clinkers, similar to lava rocks, that are ground up to make cement. The kilns are effective because they are large, often longer than a football field, and reach temperatures of over 2,600° F (1,427° C). These kilns have the highest rate of destruction of any device tested because of the heat, turbulence, and length of time that the waste is exposed to the heat. As an added benefit, there is no ash. The inorganic substances that don't burn become part of the cement and are in a form that is no longer harmful. These kilns may burn hazardous wastes, such as flammable solvents, paint and coating wastes, and printing inks. They do not burn toxic wastes such as PCBs.

Stabilization. Wastes that cannot be incinerated, such as heavy metals and toxic incinerator ash, can be chemically stabilized and solidified by mixing them with one or more ingredients, such as Portland cement or asphalt. This can prevent toxic chemicals from leaching out into the environment.

Landfilling. The most common method of disposing of toxic waste is to place it in a secure landfill. These landfills have thick clay or plastic linings to hold in the waste. The leachate is collected and treated to remove the poisons. Unfortunately, this method of disposal doesn't do anything to neutralize or destroy the poisons; it just stores them away. Furthermore, even the best landfills may have flaws that might eventually produce leaks. The clay or plastic linings can crack, allowing the leachate to drain into the earth and possibly into water supplies. Even though these landfills are now monitored to detect any leakage, most toxic substances can remain poisonous for centuries, long after the monitoring has stopped. The federal government is developing standards for minimum treatment required before wastes may be landfilled.

WASTE-EATING BACTERIA

Perhaps the most exciting technology in dealing with toxic waste involves the use of bacteria, or microbes, to gobble up toxins. Naturally occurring bacteria are treated to enhance their toxic-waste destructive properties. These mutant microbes, or "bugs," can destroy many pollutants once considered impossible to degrade, including PCBs containing dioxins. This method has the advantage of allowing toxic wastes to be disposed of on-site, eliminating the potential dangers involved in transporting them.

Microbiologist James Whitlock, of the Homestake Mining Co., developed bacteria that would eat cyanide that had contaminated South Dakota's Whitewood Creek. He put billions of his "superbugs" on each of the forty-eight rotating discs in a water-treatment plant. In addition to eating the cyanide, the sticky body surfaces of the bacteria pick up zinc, iron, and other metals in the water as it passes over the plates.

Naturally occurring bacteria are also being used to break down waste into water and carbon dioxide in a lagoon that was used as a chemical dump near Houston, Texas. Oxygen and nutrients are pumped into the lagoon to help the waste-eating microbes flourish. The mixture is stirred continuously. It is estimated that it will cost $40 to $50 million and take three to four years for the microbes to clean the 80,000 cubic yards of contaminated soil and sand in the lagoon. If the same job were done in an incinerator, the cleanup would cost an estimated $140 million and take four to six years to complete.

Another method of cleaning up toxic waste is still in the experimental stage, but it is showing promise. A Chicago research group has had success zapping contaminated sites with low-frequency radio waves. This method literally cooks the wastes so that they evaporate out of the soil. A bed of charcoal filters over the site collects the toxic vapors for later removal. Researchers claim they can clean up polluted sites for roughly $30 to $50 a ton, compared with the typical $150 per ton for carting and then incinerating soil.

INFECTIOUS WASTE

Hospitals and medical laboratories have wastes that are dangerous because of their infectious nature. Most people were not particularly concerned with these wastes until vials of blood, syringes, used bandages, and similar items began washing onto beaches during the summer of 1988. The fear of AIDS has also made people more concerned about how these wastes are being disposed of.

The ninety-two hospitals in New York City generate some 150 million pounds (68 million kg) of medical waste each year. Up to a quarter of this waste is infectious. Although the hospitals have their own regulations for disposal of these wastes, those from doctors' offices and clinics are more likely to be overlooked.

Until recently, there was no government control over medical waste as there was for other types of hazardous waste. Municipalities have their own regulations. Most require that infectious waste be burned in special high-temperature incinerators or buried in special landfills. But the fear that some medical wastes were being dumped illegally prompted the federal government to step in. At the end of 1988, the Medical Waste Tracking Act was passed. It gave the EPA six months to develop a two-year trial program that would track medical wastes in certain states. The new regulations set up by this act would keep track of all medical wastes from the place where they were generated to their final disposal site.

NUCLEAR WASTE

Nuclear waste is the most long-lasting and toxic waste that human beings have managed to create. It is dangerous because it is radioactive; it produces invisible radiation that can kill or damage any cell that it comes in contact with. Sometimes these damaged cells can cause cancer. If a reproductive cell is exposed to radiation, genetic damage that can be transmitted to future generations may result. In extreme cases, such as the accident at the Chernobyl nuclear energy plant in the USSR, the amount of radiation can be great enough to cause death.

Nuclear waste is not only dangerous, it remains that way for an incredibly long time. Some experts think that radioactive waste needs to be stored for 300 to 500 years before it will reach a low enough level of radiation to be considered safe. Others think the waste may remain dangerous for millions of years. One reason for the discrepancy is that one substance may differ from another in its half-life—the time it takes to lose 50 percent of its radioactivity by decay. Some of the more commonly used materials have half-lives of about thirty years, compared to plutonium, with an estimated half-life of 24,000 years.

The method of disposing of nuclear waste depends upon its type. *High-level waste* comes from the production of nuclear weapons and from the generation of electricity in nuclear energy plants. This type of waste generates a lot of heat and requires cooling with large amounts of water and heavy shielding with materials such as concrete and lead to keep the radiation from harming anyone.

Low-level waste comes mainly from institutions that use radioactive materials, such as hospitals, laboratories, nuclear power plants, and industrial plants. Low-level waste includes contaminated clothing, rags and paper towels, medical treatment and research materials, and other mildly radioactive materials. Currently, all permanent disposal of low-level waste is in specially designed trenches about 25 feet (9 m) deep.

Much of the high-level nuclear waste that must be disposed of is in the spent (used) fuel from nuclear energy plants. Spent fuel is highly radioactive and generates a lot of heat. Rods containing the spent fuel are usually submerged in large pools of water at power plants. Storing them in water cools them and keeps their radioactivity contained. Some of these pools are filling up rapidly.

There is still no permanent solution for disposing of high-level nuclear waste. It is generally solidified into a glass or ceramic form and sealed into metal canisters. Spent fuel is already in ceramic form, so it does not have to be solidified. Once the waste is prepared, a suitable spot must be found for its final burial.

For more than thirty years, research has been conducted to determine where high-level nuclear waste can be stored permanently. Most scientists think that the safest way to dispose of nuclear waste is to bury it in very deep rock formations that are not expected to shift or change for thousands of years. In this way, the glass that the waste is solidified in, the metal canister that holds the waste, the packing material around the canister, and the geological formation itself would all act as barriers to keep radiation from escaping.

Other scientists are skeptical about burial. They believe that there is no way to predict the stability of a rock formation over thousands of years. And if the rocks around the buried waste do shift, no packaging will withstand the resulting stress and strain. Also, some radioactive substances will be dangerous for more than ten thousand years.

Another alternative being studied is to bury the waste in geologic formations beneath the ocean floor. Scientists have identified some potential sites in the North Pacific and the North Atlantic that are considered to be very stable geologically. In these isolated spots the ocean is roughly 10,000 to 16,000 thousand feet deep (3,000 to 5,000 m), the seafloor is flat, and the sediments are thick and uniform over a large area.

The difficulty involved in disposing of nuclear waste has led to more interest in reducing the amount of waste generated in the first place. There is also interest in reducing the volume of that waste after it has been generated. This can be done by compaction, incineration, filtration, and evaporation. These methods could extend the operating life of present disposal sites, as well as cut down on the need for interim storage and transportation of the waste.

A WORLDWIDE PROBLEM

Disposing of hazardous waste is a worldwide problem, affecting even countries that generate little or no hazardous wastes of their own. In 1987 and 1988, some 3 million tons of hazardous waste were shipped from the United States and Western Europe to countries in Africa and Eastern Europe. This has caused some people in

Third World countries to claim that their countries are being used as hazardous waste dumps by richer nations. Some of this waste has been dumped carelessly. In 1988, an Italian company disposed of eight thousand leaking drums of highly toxic waste on a Nigerian farm near a schoolyard.

World leaders are finally addressing the problem of hazardous waste. More than a hundred countries got together in 1989 and drew up a treaty to restrict the shipments of hazardous waste across borders. The purpose of the treaty was to prevent the exportation of hazardous waste to unsafe, unsuitable sites. It would require waste exporters to notify and receive permission from receiving countries before shipping waste. It would also require the countries shipping the waste, as well as those receiving it, to insure that the waste will be discarded in an environmentally safe manner. The treaty is weaker than some countries would like, but it is at least a step in the right direction. It will go into effect when it is ratified by twenty countries.

GOVERNMENT ACTIONS AND HAZARDOUS WASTE

In an effort to protect Americans from the hazardous waste they produce, Congress passed the Resource Conservation and Recovery Act in 1976. RCRA regulates the transportation, treatment, storage, and disposal of hazardous waste in the United States.

Before RCRA set standards for how hazardous waste should be handled, about 90 percent of it was disposed of in ways that could harm human health and the environment. Most wastes were not treated to make them less hazardous. Liquid wastes, sludges, and slurries (thin mixtures of liquids and solids) were usually dumped into

110

pits or lagoons. Most of these had no type of lining to keep the wastes from seeping into the ground. Other hazardous wastes were dumped into landfills that were not designed for that purpose.

The regulations set forth by RCRA require manufacturers to first determine if their waste is hazardous. If hazardous waste is to be kept on the property where it is generated, the producer must obtain a permit to operate a hazardous waste treatment, storage, or disposal facility. Any waste leaving the property is closely monitored. All containers must be clearly identified as to their contents and their destination. Only haulers with EPA identification numbers are allowed to transport hazardous waste and the waste can only be shipped to facilities with permits from the state or EPA. Once the waste reaches its destination, the producer is notified within 30 days. If the producer isn't notified, he or she informs the EPA or the state so it can begin an investigation. In this way, hazardous waste is regulated from "cradle-to-grave."

Although RCRA set up the requirements for how hazardous waste should be disposed of, it didn't provide any money to clean up the sites where hazardous substances had been dumped improperly before those regulations went into effect. In 1980, the EPA established the Superfund to take up where RCRA leaves off. It provides the money to do whatever is needed to protect the environment. It also has the authority to make those who have created the problem help pay for its cleanup.

Superfund began with $1.6 billion in federal money to be used to clean up the most dangerous abandoned waste dump sites. The money came from a tax on crude oil and petroleum products. According to the plan, when dangerous sites are identified, money is taken from the fund for cleanup. The companies responsible for the wastes are expected to repay the government for the cleanup operation. That money would go back into the Superfund to be used for the next site. This way, the responsible parties end up paying the bill.

As with many plans, Superfund has not worked out as well as expected. The fund was created as a short-term solution to the problem of hazardous waste dumps, but the problem is too large to be taken care of quickly. Between the time Superfund was enacted, in 1980, and early 1989, only forty-three toxic waste dumps had been cleaned up at a staggering cost of $4 million. The process is very slow. Even after a site makes it onto the most-dangerous list, it is often seven to nine years before actual cleanup can even begin. Once the job is started, it usually takes two to three years to complete. Experts estimate that 10,000 sites may eventually need work at a total cost of more than $300 billion.

Superfund has angered many people. Environmentalists think that the process takes much too long. Many of the companies that are being made to pay for the cleanup feel that they are being unjustly punished since they dumped their wastes in a manner that followed the regulations at that time. An even bigger complaint is that the honest companies who are admitting their guilt are ending up paying for the cleanup of many dishonest dumpers who refuse to pay anything.

There are some ways Superfund could be changed to make it more effective. First, the EPA should work faster to evaluate the sites to determine which ones present an immediate danger to public health or to the environment. It should then work quickly to protect the environment around the worst dumps while it decides on the best long-term solution. The EPA should also work to get more cooperation from companies, possibly by rewarding the cooperative companies by sharing their cleanup costs, while using legal means to pressure non-settlers into paying their share.

Cleaning up dangerous waste sites should get better and cheaper as cleanup technologies improve and the work force becomes more experienced.

PROTECTING THE FUTURE

The earth is home to billions of people. We cannot continue to poison its air, land, and water with hazardous wastes as we did in the past. Although it is easy to blame industries for polluting our nation, the problem stems partially from the high standard of living Americans enjoy. This life-style depends on a tremendous number of products, many of which produce hazardous wastes during the manufacturing process. Along with our desire to keep and improve our standard of living comes the responsibility of finding a safe way to dispose of the hazardous by-products our life-style creates. We must be prepared to pay the higher costs involved in disposing of our hazardous waste in ways that prevent damage to human health and the environment.

113

8

CONQUERING
THE MOUNTAIN

THE ETERNAL PROBLEM

As long as there are people on the earth there will be a problem disposing of the wastes they create. In the United States, where the convenience of throwing things away has become a way of life, the problem may become insurmountable if changes are not made.

Our country is not suffering from a lack of technology, but rather from a lack of willingness to accept what must be done to solve the solid-waste crisis. Since our "throwaway society" is basically a cultural problem, it may take cultural changes to solve it. For instance, Americans will have to form the habit of recycling some of their waste instead of tossing everything out and forgetting about it. They may have to get used to leaving the grass clippings on their lawns or having a compost pile in the backyard to cut down on the tons of yard wastes thrown out each year.

Some idealists suggest that we go back to a simpler life with less packaging and fewer throwaway items, but this is not likely to happen. Americans are not about to give up their disposable diapers and TV dinners. The alternative is to find better ways of dealing with the mountains of garbage that are the price we must pay for our standard of living.

Progress in solving the solid-waste crisis has been slowed in part by the differing views of several special-interest groups. Environmental groups, consultants, manufacturers, government agencies, politicians, and homeowners are all at odds with each other over how our waste problems should be solved. The waste-to-energy companies are afraid that an emphasis on recycling will not leave them enough solid waste to fuel their furnaces. Scrap dealers worry that recyclers will steal their business. The plastic manufacturers worry that government regulations will limit their growth. Homeowners don't want landfills or resource-recovery facilities placed anywhere near them. The environmentalists want EPA regulations to be stricter, while businesses want the EPA to stop making such costly regulations. It seems as if there is no way to please everyone. But until communities are willing to pay for building adequate facilities and are willing to make concessions as to where those facilities will be built, our piles of trash will continue to build up.

CUTTING IT
DOWN TO SIZE

America will never solve its solid-waste dilemma without developing programs that deal with the root of the problem—the amount of waste generated. Once the garbage has been mixed together in a dumpster or trash truck, the options of what can be done with that garbage are limited. It can be either placed in a landfill or burned. More attention must be given to the garbage before it is thrown out. This can be done through the 3Rs of source reduction—*reduce, reuse, recycle.*

The most obvious way to solve the garbage problem

is to produce less garbage to begin with. Reducing the amount of packaging our products come in would help. The amount of packaging we throw away has increased 80 percent since 1960 and now makes up a third of household trash. Reducing the waste stream also can be accomplished by discontinuing the use of certain products, by making products more durable so they will not need to be replaced as often, and by encouraging manufacturers to decrease the amount of waste generated during the manufacturing process.

Another method of source reduction is to reuse items, such as returnable bottles, instead of throwing them away. Many states now have bottle deposit laws to encourage the reuse of these containers. Even garage and yard sales or the donation of used items to charities can result in the reuse of products that are still good.

The third "R" in source reduction is recycling. Some experts believe that as much as 80 percent of our waste stream could be recycled, yet the United States presently only recycles about 10 percent of its waste. Successful recycling programs will require the cooperation of those generating the waste and good markets for the recycled products.

MORE RESEARCH NEEDED

The main goal of any solid-waste management strategy is to provide for the disposal of waste in ways that have the least impact on human health and the environment. Although some progress is being made, research is still needed in several areas to achieve this goal.

In the area of landfills, research is needed to find better, more durable landfill liners and caps. Since leachate can be a problem, there need to be better methods of analyzing water samples for indications of contamination and better methods of treating leachate to re-

117

Industries and individuals can reduce the amount of waste in the world by reusing or recycling many items that are thrown away.

move or neutralize dangerous contaminants. More efficient ways of recovering methane are also needed.

Right now there is no evidence that properly run resource-recovery facilities pose any health hazard to humans, but many people are still suspicious of them. More research is needed to answer unresolved questions about resource-recovery facilities and to instill more confidence in their safety. Research may provide a better understanding of the formation of furans, dioxins, and other potentially dangerous substances, so that methods can be developed to eliminate or control them. The research presently being conducted is expected to bring refinements in incineration technology, emission-control technology, and diagnostic monitoring techniques.

More research is needed to assess the dangers of toxic substances that end up in our waste stream. The EPA has listed more than 48,000 chemicals, yet almost nothing is currently known about the toxic effects of almost 38,000 of them. Until more money is spent on research to know the effect of these substances, we will not know how to handle them in the safest manner possible.

Presently in the United States there is no ocean dumping of municipal solid waste. However, considering the shortage of landfill space in our country as well as other industrialized nations, ocean dumping of some municipal solid wastes or incinerator ash may have to be looked at more closely. Because of the complex nature of oceans, extensive research would be needed to find methods that would not disrupt the ecosystem of the ocean or threaten human health. By researching the biological and chemical interactions of different stabilized waste materials with each other and with the environment, scientists may find cases where ocean dumping would be acceptable. Protecting the oceans would require national and international diagnostic monitoring systems to quickly detect and trace any pollution.

THE FUTURE OF WASTE DISPOSAL

By the turn of the century millions of Americans will be obligated by law to separate recyclable materials out of their trash. As time goes on, more cities will burn a larger portion of their refuse in resource-recovery facilities. In many areas landfills will be used more for the disposal of incinerator ash than for raw garbage.

There is much room for improvement in our solid-waste disposal system, but it won't be cheap. The problem may not be solved until there are economic incentives strong enough to get manufacturers to use fewer materials; for garbage collectors to limit the waste they pick up; or for consumers to cut back on the amount they throw away. It is going to take a joint effort by individuals, communities, and businesses to accept the responsibility for limiting waste production. If this is not done, we may soon reach a point where we can no longer afford to support our throwaway society.

GLOSSARY

AEROBE—A microorganism that lives only in the presence of oxygen.

ANAEROBE—A microorganism that lives in the absence of oxygen.

BAGHOUSE—A unit containing several porous bags that can filter fine particles out of incinerator smoke.

BIODEGRADABLE—Capable of decaying or being broken down by the actions of microorganisms.

CULLET—Crushed glass used in the manufacture of new glass.

DIOXIN—A toxic chemical created as a by-product of the manufacture of certain weed killers and other industrial processes.

ELECTROSTATIC PRECIPITATORS—Electrically charged metal plates used to remove fly ash from incinerator smoke.

FLY ASH—Fine particles of ashes, soot, and dust found in the smoke given off by burning refuse in an incinerator.

LEACHATE—A solution produced by water dissolving contaminants as it seeps through landfills.

METHANE—A flammable gas produced by the rotting of biodegradable wastes.

MICROORGANISMS—Living beings, such as bacteria, too tiny to be seen by the unaided eye.

NONBIODEGRADABLE—Not capable of decaying or being broken down.

PCB—Polychlorinated biphenyl. Synthetic organic compounds that become harmful pollutants when released into the environment.

RDF (REFUSE-DERIVED FUEL)—A fuel burned in specialized boilers that is made by shredding refuse from which glass and metal have been removed.

SCRUBBER—A device used for removing impurities from gases given off during the burning of refuse in an incinerator.

SLUDGE—A muddy or slushy mass such as the solid matter that separates out during water- and sewage-treatment processes.

TOXIC—A substance that is poisonous or causes cancer.

TRANSFER STATION—A facility where refuse from smaller collection trucks is transferred to larger vehicles for long-distance hauling.

FOR FURTHER READING

Hawkes, Nigel. *Toxic Waste and Recycling*. New York: Gloucester Press, 1988.

Kiefer, Irene. *Poisoned Land*. New York: Atheneum, 1981.

Miller, Christina G., and Louise A. Berry. *Wastes*. New York: Franklin Watts, 1986.

Pringle, Laurence. *Throwing Things Away*. New York: Crowell, 1986.

Weiss, Malcolm E. *Toxic Waste*. New York: Franklin Watts, 1984.

Woods, Geraldine, and Harold Woods. *Pollution*. New York: Franklin Watts, 1985.

INDEX

Long-distance shipping, 26–28
Love Canal, 97–98

MARPOL treaty, 95
Mass-burn facilities, 54–55
Methane gas, 38–40, 44, 47
Morris, David, 68

National Coalition for Recyclable Waste, 76
Niagara Falls, NY, 97–98
NIMBY syndrome, 17–19, 35, 60–61
Nuclear wastes, 107–109

Obsolescence, 14
Oceans:
dumping in, 87–94, 119–120
importance of, 90–92
incineration in, 92, 95
for nuclear waste, 109
protection of, 95–96

Packaging, 14–15
Paper, 61, 78–80
Parks, 45–47
PCBs, 57, 95, 103
PET bottles, 82
Pit stations, 26
Plastic:
decaying of, 37

and incineration, 49
for leachate, 42–43
ocean dumping of, 95
recycling of, 81–83
Pollution:
and incineration, 56–58
ocean, 91
of water, 40–44
Population, 14, 88
PVC, recycling of, 81

Radio waves, 106
Radioactive wastes, 107–109
RCRA (Resource Conservation and Recovery Act), 77, 110–111
RDF (refuse-derived fuel), 55
Recycling, 19, 22, 65–66, 116–118
and composting, 84–86
examples of, 77–84
implementation of, 71–72
improvements in, 72–77
and incineration, 61
need for, 67–68
problems with, 68–71
of toxic wastes, 101, 103
Reduction of waste, 101–102, 116–118